The
ROMAN
MYSTERIES
QUIZ BOOK

To find out more about
the Roman Mysteries, visit

www.romanmysteries.com

THE ROMAN MYSTERIES
by *Caroline Lawrence*

Look out for . . .

THE SECOND ROMAN MYSTERIES QUIZ BOOK

Caroline Lawrence

Orion
Children's Books

First published in Great Britain in 2007
by Orion Children's Books
a division of the Orion Publishing Group Ltd
Orion House
5 Upper St Martin's Lane
London WC2H 9EA

1 3 5 7 9 10 8 6 4 2

A catalogue record for this book is available from the British Library

ISBN 978 1 84255 595 8

Printed in Great Britain by Clays Ltd, St Ives plc

www.orionbooks.co.uk

CONTENTS

WELCOME!

If I had a time machine, and could go back to any period in the past, it would be Roman times. I would give any-thing to know what it was really like to go to the baths, witness a gladiator fight, watch a chariot race . . . I would love to know what first century Rome smelled like, felt like, tasted like. And what it *really* looked like. Sadly, nobody has yet invented a time machine, so I can't go back.

But if someone could fill a book with accurate facts about ancient Rome – as well as vivid descriptions of the sights and smells and tastes –wouldn't that be almost as good as a time machine? That's what I've tried to do in The Roman Mysteries. How do I know what it looked and smelled and tasted like? By visiting the ancient sites, going to museums, reading books, studying their ancient languages and dressing up like a Roman. In so doing, I've collected tons of facts and artefacts. My Roman Mysteries are full of them. So is this Quiz Book.

Artefacts are the things that people used in past times. The Latin word 'artefact' means 'something made by skill'. Artefacts reveal the sight and feel and smell and sound of the ancient world. A glass chariot beaker, with moulded charioteers racing round the central barrier of the Circus Maximus, is the ancient equivalent of a souvenir mug you might buy at your team's stadium gift-shop. It even tells us the names of some ancient charioteers. A cold bronze bleeding-cup makes us shiver, as we imagine our own lifeblood filling it up. It was the ancient equivalent of paracetamol. A statue thrusting its hand palm outwards shows us what one of the signs against evil looked like. It was the ancient equivalent of knocking on wood or crossing yourself.

I get some of my facts about ancient Rome from modern historians but most I get from the writings of the ancient Romans themselves. For example, we have an eyewitness account of the opening of the Colosseum from a poet called Martial. We have accounts of chariot races, including one which describes the horses' legs 'crackling in the spokes of the wheels' during a terrible crash. We have philosophical accounts in which the wise men of old discuss whether it is better to remain aloof from the pleasures of this world, or to embrace them wholeheartedly. Some of these philosophers were very dull. Roman writers could also be clever, witty and funny. The more I read, the more I suspect the Romans were just like us.

For example, today most people support a football team, and proudly wear its colours to a match. If your star player leaves, then you are sad but you are still faithful to your team. In ancient Roman times, it was exactly the same with chariot racing. If you supported the Greens, and your star charioteer got sold to the Reds, you would be sad. But you would continue to support the Greens.

Sometimes people say to me, 'Oh, we're not like the Romans. They were so barbaric. They liked to watch people die horribly in the arena.' But today's films give us a far more visceral view of blood, gore and death than the best seat in the arena ever did. And we love it!

So, as you consider the facts and artefacts in this book, and as you learn more about real life in ancient Rome, ask yourself: 'Am I really so different from them? How would I survive if I was suddenly transported to ancient Rome?'

I would like to thank the four fans, young and old(er), who helped me think up the questions for this quiz book. I would like to thank my husband Richard for his delightful drawings of a ship, a Roman Villa and the Circus Maximus. I would especially like to thank my editor Jon, who is always cheerful and patient.

Finally, I would like to thank Peter Sutton, who has not only produced a succession of exciting book covers for the Roman Mysteries series, but has here taken my photos and clippings of Roman artefacts, and has transformed them into clear and attractive illustrations, so you can know what things really looked like in Roman times.

Vale! (farewell) Caroline

MAP QUIZZES

In every Roman Mystery there are maps at the front to show you where the story's action takes place. Can you match the place name to the letter that appears beside it on the map?

ROMAN MERCHANT SHIP

1. Altar   *Answer:* ....
2. Anchor   *Answer:* ....
3. Artemon   *Answer:* ....
4. Deck-house   *Answer:* ....
5. Halyard   *Answer:* ....
6. Hull   *Answer:* ....
7. Lifts   *Answer:* ....
8. Mainmast   *Answer:* ....
9. Steering oars   *Answer:* ....
10. Tiller   *Answer:* ....

For the answers to these questions, turn to page 134.

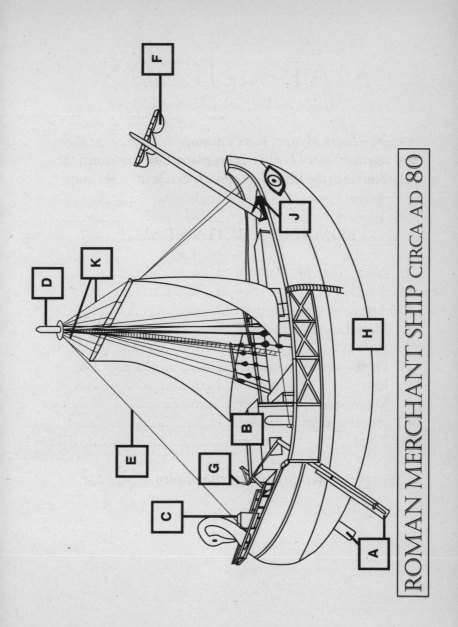

ROMAN MERCHANT SHIP CIRCA AD 80

VILLA OF POLLIUS FELIX

11. Atrium   Answer: ....
12. Baths   Answer: ....
13. Entrance to the
    Secret Cove   Answer: ....
14. Library Tower   Answer: ....
15. Ornamental pool   Answer: ....
16. Shrine of Venus   Answer: ....
17. Slave quarters   Answer: ....
18. Stables   Answer: ....
19. Statue of Felix   Answer: ....
20. Terrace   Answer: ....

For the answers to these questions, turn to page 134.

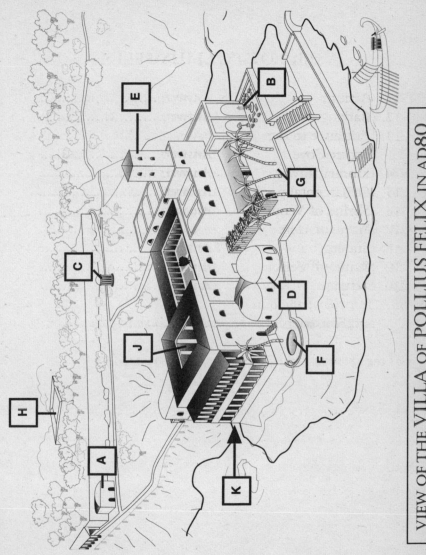

VIEW OF THE VILLA OF POLLIUS FELIX IN AD80

CIRCUS MAXIMUS

21. Carceres
    (starting gates)   *Answer:* ....
22. Dolphin markers   *Answer:* ....
23. Egg markers   *Answer:* ....
24. Linea alba   *Answer:* ....
25. Meta prima   *Answer:* ....
26. Obelisk of Augustus   *Answer:* ....
27. Shrine of Consus
    (underground)   *Answer:* ....
28. Shrine of Murcia   *Answer:* ....
29. Statue of Victory   *Answer:* ....
30. Temple of the Sun
    and Finishing Box   *Answer:* ....

For the answers to these questions, turn to page 135.

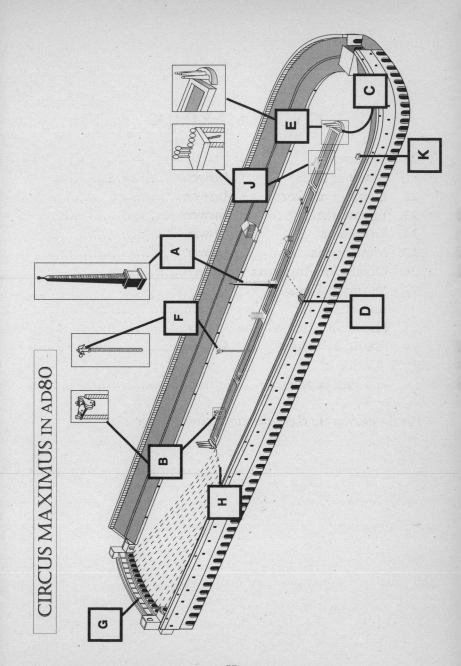

CIRCUS MAXIMUS IN AD80

THE ENEMIES
OF JUPITER

Prometheus, bound, has his liver pecked by a vulture.
(Illustration based on a black-figure vase from c.530 BC)

31. In the opening scroll of *The Enemies of Jupiter*, what kind of meat does Jonathan accidentally burn while cooking his father's birthday dinner?

32. Why did Mordecai ask his daughter Miriam not to attend his birthday dinner party in fever-ravaged Ostia?

33. Which ONE of the following is NOT a diagnostic method used by Doctor Mordecai when he and Jonathan examine the widow Helena Aurelia?
    A. Asking her to say what's bothering her
    B. Asking her to stick out her tongue
    C. Taking her temperature
    D. Observing the general colour of her complexion

34. Which ONE of the following is NOT an ingredient of Doctor Mordecai's special elixir?
    A. Marjoram
    B. Poppy Tears
    C. Turpentine
    D. Honey

35. In the upstairs storeroom of Jonathan's house, in Mordecai's medicine cabinet, is a large, greyish-white cylinder. According to Mordecai, it is extremely expensive and rare. What is it?

36. Flavia's great-grandfather made his fortune trading in which ONE of the following?
    A. Salt
    B. Sugar

C. Silver

D. Slaves

37. Aristo says that tragedy warns us against hubris.
What is his two-word definition of hubris?

38. The Romans believed there were four physical
types, based on an excess of one of the four
humours in the body. Which ONE of the following
was NOT one of the four humours?
A. Blood
B. Water
C. Phlegm
D. Yellow Bile
E. Black Bile

39. Which of Mordecai's medical instruments does
Nubia mistake for a bronze goat-bell, 'but with no
bell noise'?

40. Each of the four humours is associated with one
of the four elements. According to Lupus, which
element goes with choleric types, like Nubia?

41. Jonathan and his friends receive an invitation to
dinner on their first night in the Imperial Palace.
The man with bushy eyebrows who delivers the
invitation is someone Jonathan has met before.
Who?

42. Beside the Imperial Palace on the Palatine Hill
stands the Temple of Apollo. From here Flavia
and her friends can see the Circus Maximus, the

Roman forum, and – on a hill opposite – the Temple of Jupiter Optimus Maximus. On what hill does that temple stand?

43. Directly behind the Temple of Apollo is the imperial library, two colonnades full of scrolls. One is full of scrolls in Greek. What language are the scrolls in the facing colonnade?

44. Titus's long-haired slave-boys wear a perfume which was very popular in first century Rome. Today we use it as a spice. What is it?

45. Titus gives each of the detectives small rectangular imperial passes, giving them access to all areas. Of what material are these rectangular passes?

46. Which sacred animals – which once raised the alarm against approaching barbarians – live on the Capitoline Hill?

47. What was the name of the rocky part of the Capitoline Hill from which traitors were thrown?

48. In the library housed in the Temple of Apollo, Flavia and her friends meet a freedman of the Emperor who is writing a history of the Jewish people. They have met him before. What is the name of this famous Jewish historian?

49. Which landmark of Rome does Nubia first mistake for a 'boat with trees and temples on it'?

50. The original Sibylline books – foretelling Rome's future – were destroyed in a fire on the Capitoline Hill. According to Ascletario, which Roman emperor tried to reconstruct them?

51. According to Titus's astrologer, Ascletario, the replacement books of prophecy are kept in a golden box in a temple on the Palatine Hill at the foot of the statue of which god?

52. The young apothecary on the Tiber Island keeps his pet – called Ptolemy – in a circular basket. What kind of creature is Ptolemy?

53. At one point, Titus's own daughter falls ill with the fever. What is her name?

54. What holy relic from Jerusalem does Jonathan believe he has found in Nero's Golden House?

55. Hebrew letters are also numbers. Whose name – when written in Hebrew – adds up to 666, the number of The Beast?

56. The friends agree to rendezvous at the library in the Temple of Apollo on the Palatine Hill. If for any reason one of them can't make it on time, the others will leave a message in code. The code will be Latin written backwards but in a different alphabet. Which alphabet?

57. As Josephus is struck down by the fever, he begins to rant. Which ONE of the following animals does he NOT mention in his delirium?
    A. Kitten
    B. Puppy
    C. Buzzing flies
    D. Rock badger

58. When Mordecai and the young detectives are ejected from the Imperial Palace, they seek refuge with Flavia's aunt and uncle? What is the name of Flavia's aunt?

59. As proof of God's wrath against Titus, Agathus lists the disasters that have befallen Rome since he came to power. Which ONE of the following does Agathus NOT mention?
    A. The volcano
    B. The giant wave caused by the volcano
    C. The blighted harvest
    D. The blood red sunsets
    E. The pestilence

60. When Flavia thinks she sees the sun rising in the west – what is she really seeing?

For the answers to these questions, turn to page 135.

ENTERTAINMENT IN ROMAN TIMES

61. Which Latin word beginning with 'N' and meaning 'shipwreck!' did people shout when a chariot crashed in the hippodrome?

62. In a chariot race of four bigae from each faction, how many horses are involved?

63. Historians estimate that first century Rome had a million residents. They believe the Flavian amphi-theatre (now known as the Colosseum) could seat fifty thousand people. According to some historians, how many people did the Circus Maximus hold?

64. Ancient Roman games and modern Spanish bull-fights have all the following things in common except one. Which one?
    A. Important personage sits in the best seat
    B. A procession before the main events
    C. Cushions and snacks sold by vendors
    D. Music played during the events
    E. Handkerchiefs waved to show approval
    F. Execution of criminals during breaks between events
    G. Dead animals dragged off with hooks
    H. Bloody sand raked over to make it look clean again

65. Scholars believe that Domitian added underfloor cells to the Colosseum about ten years after it was first opened by Titus. Until then, it could be flooded for special water events, as in *The Gladiators from Capua*. Where else in Rome could people watch water events, like sea-fights?

66. In first century Rome one of the most famous celebrities was a handsome young beast-fighter. What was his name?

67. For a short time in the late first century, Domitian tried to introduce two new colours to the chariot-racing factions: Gold and Purple. These never caught on. Which ONE of the following was NEVER a colour of the chariot racing factions?
A. Orange
B. Red
C. White
D. Blue
E. Green

68. The more prominent a person in Roman society, the nearer they sat to the Emperor at the games. Which of the following groups sat closest to the Imperial Box?
A. Wealthy foreigners
B. Equestrians
C. Senators
D. Merchants

69. What is a venatrix?

70. Which type of gladiator – known as a 'net-man' – fought with a trident, dagger and net, but no helmet?

71. Which type of gladiator – known as a 'fish-man' – fought with a sword, shield and greaves, and often had a fish on his helmet?

72. In chariot-racing, what name is given to the right-hand yoke horse, who occupies the most important position?

73. Which ONE of the following would a victorious gladiator NOT receive?
A. A palm branch
B. A victory wreath
C. A bag of gold
D. A steel sword

74. According to Bar-Mnason – and modern statistics – which of the following animals is most dangerous to humans?
A. Crocodile
B. Leopard
C. Hippopotamus
D. Giraffe
F. Nubian lion

75. Someone tells Jonathan that the slaves who have been working on the Flavian amphitheatre (i.e. the Colosseum) have been building their own tomb, because they will probably be thrown to the beasts. From which conquered city are these slaves?

76. What is the minimum number of races a
    'miliarius' must win to claim the title?
    A. 100
    B. 1000
    C. 10,000
    D. A million

77. What does it signify when a gladiator raises his
    right arm with his forefinger extended?

78. In a gladiatorial match, what would the crowd cry
    when a gladiator received a hit or wound?

79. Nobody knows for certain if the sign to spare a
    gladiator was thumbs up, thumbs down, or thumbs
    in. But recent finds in Ephesus have uncovered a
    gladiators' grave-yard. Many of the skeletons have
    scratch-marks on the inside of their left collar-bone,
    indicating a swift downward blow from a short
    thrusting sword. What was the short, thrusting
    sword of the Romans called?

80. On one end of the central barrier of the Circus
    Maximus were dolphins, on the other were eggs;
    these marked off the laps. How many laps did the
    chariots run?

81. Which ONE of the following is NOT a benefit of
    a charioteer having the reins tied round his waist?
    A. It makes it easier to run off the track if he is
       thrown out of the chariot
    B. He can use his whole body to steer

C. It leaves his right hand free for the whip

D. It leaves his left hand free to twitch particular reins

82. What did Romans do to the statues of their gods and heroes in the amphitheatre, to avoid offending them with the sight of blood and violence?

83. The traditional opponent of the retiarius was a heavily-armed gladiator with a tight, smooth helmet with small round eye-holes. What was this type of gladiator called?

84. Gladiators did not always die in the arena. If a gladiator fought well, he would be sent off with his honour intact, so that he could fight another day. Which Latin word beginning with 'M' is the term for this honourable dismissal?

85. The gladiator school based in Capua was called the Ludus Julianus, after the famous Roman who founded it. Who was its founder?

86. According to Pliny the Elder's *Natural History*, some Romans were able to quickly tell friends in faraway countries which faction had won the chariot races. They did this by dipping the wings of a certain type of bird in paint the same colour as the winning faction. Which type of bird did they use?

87. Flavia's Uncle Cornix is a conservative man and does not approve of most entertainment. Which ONE of the following DOES he enjoy?
   A. The theatre
   B. Beast-fights
   C. Chariot racing
   D. Mimes and pantomimes
   E. Gladiatorial combats

88. According to Flavia's cousin Aulus, what are 'rooftiles'?

89. The *linea alba* is a white line on the race track. What are charioteers forbidden to do until they reach it?

90. Charioteers were allowed to choose their lanes in the order that balls the colour of their faction were drawn out of a revolving urn. Who selected the balls?

For the answers to these questions, turn to page 136.

LOOKING GOOD IN ROMAN TIMES

With thanks to contributing Quizmaster Errin Riley

91. At the beginning of *The Enemies of Jupiter*, Doctor Mordecai adopts a more Roman appearance to please his Roman patients. Which ONE of the following does he NOT do to achieve this new look?
    A. Stops wearing a turban
    B. Starts using hair oil
    C. Cuts his hair
    D. Shaves off his beard

92. When Nubia first sees Jonathan's mother Susannah, she is struck by her beauty and by her resemblance to Miriam, Jonathan's sister. Apart from the fact that she is sixteen years older than her daughter, what is the big difference between Susannah's appearance and Miriam's?

93. Susannah's slave-girl Delilah would be lovely, except for one thing. What?

94. Before coming to the Villa Limona, what special ingredient did Flavia add to the hot water rinse for her hair, in order to make it glossy like Miriam's?

95. When Flavia first steps off the boat and onto the docking platform of the Villa Limona, what aspect of her appearance immediately horrifies Pulchra?

96. Pulchra compliments Jonathan on how muscular he is: 'Have you been weight-lifting in the ....?'

97. Flavia is horrified by Pulchra's mirror because it 'shows every tiny spot!' In Roman times what were most mirrors made of?

98. As she gazes into the mirror, Flavia wonders aloud if her nose is too big. 'No,' says Nubia loyally, 'It is ....'

99. Flavia grumbles that whereas Nubia's eyes are 'lovely golden-brown', hers are 'dull old ....'

100. In a letter to her father, Flavia describes the young widow Claudia Casta as a 'tawny beauty with eyes like a ....'

101. In the baths of the Villa Limona, Pulchra bluntly tells Flavia that she is not beautiful and never will be. She then lists Flavia's defects. Which ONE of the following does she NOT mention?
A. Eyes too small
B. Nose too big
C. Mouth too wide
D. Knobbly knees
E. Big feet

102. In Roman times it was considered a sign of beauty for a woman to have a low forehead. According to Pulchra, Flavia's brow is
A. Too low
B. Too high
C. Just right
D. Ape-like

103. Pulchra consoles Flavia by telling her that because she is witty and clever she does not need to be beautiful. Pulchra quotes her mother Polla, who says only 'girls who are .... need to be beautiful.'

104. Pulchra tells Flavia she can allow her inner beauty to shine through by being well-groomed. Which ONE of the following does Pulchra NOT mention as an example of good grooming for a Roman female?
A. Having well-coiffed hair
B. Having smooth limbs
C. Having pale skin
D. Having fresh breath

105. Pulchra, whose name means 'beautiful', is very conscious of grooming. Which ONE of the following concoctions does she NOT have access to in *The Sirens of Surrentum*?

A. Mouthwash made of urine and wine
B. Depilatory made of turpentine and rabbits' blood
C. Hair bleach made of lye
D. Skin bleach made of lard and lemon juice
E. Lip salve of beeswax and ochre

106. The word 'depilatory' comes from two Latin words: 'hair' and 'off'. Pulchra recommends that the girls use a depilatory to take the hair off their limbs. 'You and Nubia don't want furry ...., do you?'

107. Which ONE of the following items does NOT appear in Flavia's new make-up kit?
A. Piece of slate
B. Soft chunks of coloured rock
C. Charcoal
D. Mortar
E. Pestle

108. While staying at the Villa Limona in *The Sirens of Surrentum*, which ONE of the following does Flavia NOT do to make herself look more grown-up and attractive?
A. Bathe in asses' milk
B. Wear platform shoes
C. Put on lots of make-up
D. Curl her hair with a hot bronze rod

109. According to Pulchra – and also to Pliny the Elder
– eating which ONE of the following meats will
make you more attractive?
A. Venison
B. Boar
C. Hare
D. Goat

110. During their stay at the Villa Limona, the young
detectives investigate poisons. One poisonous
plant was used to make the pupils of the eyes
very big. This was considered very attractive in
women. The Italian word for this poison means
'Beautiful Lady'. What was it?

111. When Lupus visits the opulent Baths of Nero in
Baiae, he gets a very unusual beauty treatment for
skin. With what substance is he smeared?

112. In the opulent port of Baiae, Nubia sees lots of
fashionable women. Which ONE of the following
fashion items does she NOT notice?
A. Silken tunics in jewel-like colours
B. Parasols in jewel-like colours
C. Diamond nose-studs
D. Cork-soled platform shoes
E. Gauzy scarves instead of modest pallas

113. The men of Baiae want to look good, too, and
Nubia sees that they have their own fashion
accessories. Which ONE of the following does
she NOT observe?

A. Fierce dogs with spiky collars
B. Gold-plated wrist guards
C. Gilded sandals
D. Goat-hair toupées
E. Big rings

114. Publius Pollius Felix is very good-looking. However, there is one unusual thing about his appearance, his prematurely grey hair. How old was Felix when his hair turned grey?

115. At a dinner party one evening, Felix tells a story explaining why he has grey hair: one of his ancestors insulted a goddess. Which goddess?

116. Senator Cornix's young Greek secretary Sisyphus always dresses fashionably. What colour tunic is he wearing when Flavia and her friends arrive in Rome to search for the missing racehorse, in *The Charioteer of Delphi*?
A. Taupe
B. Beige
C. Fawn
D. Pink
E. Mauve

117. On the first day of the races celebrating the *Ludi Romani*, Sisyphus wears the latest fashion accessory. What is it?

118. Sisyphus always wears a certain type of make-up to emphasize his eyes. What is it?

119. When a Roman went to the baths, he or she often took a 'bath-set'. This is a bronze or brass ring with various implements of grooming hanging from it. Which ONE of the following would probably NOT hang from this bronze ring?
A. Tweezers
B. Ear-scoop
C. Strigil
D. Oil flask
E. Towel

120. At a banquet in Sentor Cornix's house, Jonathan notices that Flavia's aunt is wearing more jewellery than usual, probably to impress their guest of honour, the star charioteer of the Greens. What is his name?

For the answers to these questions, turn to page 137.

THE GLADIATORS FROM CAPUA

Orpheus attacked by maenads.
(Illustration based on a red-figure vase of c.530 BC)

121. When *The Gladiators from Capua* begins, Nubia is laying a wreath in front of a tombstone. There is no body in the tomb; the friends believe the body lies in a mass grave in which city?

122. What is the name of the man-made island between Ostia's old and new ports where many tombs are to be found, including that of Jonathan's family?

123. Flavia gives a special speech at the tomb, praising the dead person. What do we call such a speech?

124. A boy who looks like Jonathan has been sighted in Rome, on a hill made of bits of broken amphoras. Today this hill is still visible and it is known as Mons Testaccio. What do Flavia and her friends call it?

125. Flavia's uncle, Senator Cornix, invites Flavia and her friends to Rome to watch the inaugural games at the amphitheatre. What is Senator Cornix's gentilicium (middle name)?

126. What is the name of the steep street leading down from Senator Cornix's house on the Caelian Hill?
A. Via Sacra
B. Via Ostiensis
C. Via Appia
D. Clivus Scauri

127. While the friends are in Rome, they encounter red rain, which Nubia thinks is blood. This phenomenon is still observable today. According to Flavia, what makes the raindrops appear red?

128. In the arena, gladiators do not fight animals. According to Caudex, who fights animals?

129. The smell of camel dung makes Nubia remember her date-loving camel, named after a famous oasis. What was the name of Nubia's camel, and the oasis?

130. Which Latin word beginning with 'P' is the post gladiators practised on?

131. Nubia re-encounters Mnason, the animal-trainer from Ostia. In *The Twelve Tasks of Flavia Gemina*, she helped him catch an escaped lion. What was the lion's name?

132. Which instrument, comprising giant bronze pipes, provides atmospheric sound effects and music during the games?

133. Before Domitian built the great Ludus Magnus, there was a temporary gladiator school housed in Nero's Domus Aurea. In *The Gladiators from Capua*, what is this gladiator school called?

134. A famous gladiator from Thrace lived a hundred and fifty years before this story starts. He escaped

from the gladiator school of Capua and sparked a massive slave revolt. What was his name?

135. Women and children had to sit in the highest tier of the amphitheatre because it was not considered seemly for proper Roman matrons and highborn children to see blood and violence. What does Aulus Junior call this highest level?

136. Quintus Fabius Balbus is the *magister ludi* – the organiser of the games. If the inaugural games are a success, Titus has promised Fabius a town-house in Rome and a villa in which town on the Bay of Naples?

137. Fabius used to be a Stoic, and disapproved of barbaric spectacles. But when he was forced to watch such spectacles, he was instantly captivated by the blood and gore. How would you describe an obsession?
    A. Bloodletting
    B. Bloodlust
    C. Bloodbath
    D. Bloody-mindedness

138. On the first day of the amphitheatre's inaugural games, what show-stopping act concludes the tightrope-walkers' pre-games warm-up?

139. The rabbit who faces the lion in single combat is called Saevus. What does Saevus mean?

140. Mnason dyes the animals' fur dark so they can be seen against the pale sand from a great height. What natural substance does he use for dye?

141. The Latin word for scoundrel is furcifer. The word 'furcifer' means someone who wears a ....?

142. During the games, criminals were sometimes executed during breaks in the main programme. These executions were often educational as well as entertaining, illustrating characters from plays and mythology. For example, Laureolus was a real person who was depicted in a play. He was tied to a cross and gored by what animal?

143. During the games, the emperor occasionally scattered lottery balls among the spectators. Flavia tells Nubia that the hollow balls contain tokens for either a fabulous gift or a joke gift. Which ONE of the following does Flavia NOT mention as an example?
   A. A villa
   B. A basket of chickpeas
   C. A ship
   D. A toothpick
   E. A sponge-on-a-stick
   F. A slave

144. What does Flavia use to muzzle an attacking crocodile?

145. During the games, Titus's younger brother Domitian saves the lives of Nubia and Flavia, thanks to his skill at what?

146. When Flavia and Nubia go to see Domitian in the imperial box, they meet a senator called Calvus and also a rather hairy poet. This poet later wrote the Liber Spectaculorum, an eyewitness account of the opening games of the Colosseum in AD 80. What is the poet's name?

147. What happens when Titus's daughter inspects the gladiators' weapons for sharpness?

148. What causes a rainbow to appear in the arena on the second day of the games?

149. Nubia discovers that her brother Taharqo is a gladiator from the school of Capua and that he will fight in the arena. What name does he go by?

150. What is the name of the six foot tall gladiator who has six fingers on each hand and six toes on each foot?

For the answers to these questions, turn to page 138.

KILL OR CURE

151. Each of the four humours is associated with one of the four seasons. According to Jonathan, which season goes with pink-cheeked sanguine types, like Flavia?

152. The poet Martial wrote a witty poem about a doctor who killed so many of his patients that he became an undertaker. In *The Enemies of Jupiter*, Nubia meets this doctor while he is still practising medicine. Most of his patients are deathly ill because he believes blood is bad and drains them nearly dry. What is his name?

153. The poet Martial wrote several poems about a well-known Roman perfume-maker. In *The Enemies of Jupiter*, Flavia meets him while he is trying out medicine as a career. Thanks to a huge nose, he has an acute sense of smell and is quite successful as a doctor. What is his name?

154. The poet Catullus wrote a witty poem about a Spaniard called Egnatius who used a certain liquid to bleach his teeth. In *The Enemies of Jupiter*, Lupus meets a doctor – also called Egnatius – who believes this same liquid to be a panacea or 'cure-all'. What is the notorious liquid?

155. Like many Roman doctors, Egnatius believes that food is medicine. Which ONE of the following does he NOT recommend for Lupus's diet?
A. Cabbage
B. Raw onion
C. Cheese

156. Apollo is a god of plague as well as a god of healing. In the former role, he is often accompanied by a mouse. What is the Greek word for 'mouse' – and also the name of the young apothecary that Jonathan meets on the Tiber Island?

157. The Emperor Titus suffers from bad headaches. Which ONE of the following does he NOT specifically mention as something which brings him relief?
A. Letting blood
B. Drinking wine
C. Listening to music

158. A popular tonic in Roman times was called 'hydromel' after the Greek words for its two ingredients. One of the two ingredients was honey. What was the other?

159. Doctor Mordecai's treatment of those with fever proved effective in Ostia. When he goes to Rome, which ONE of the following does he NOT recommend as treatment for the ill?
A. Rest in a well-ventilated room
B. Bled every other day

C. Wine taken every other day
D. Broth taken daily
E. Prayer
F. Inhale the steam from boiled herbs

160. In claiming to be the best doctor in Rome, Cosmus adheres to the five principles of Asclepiades. Which ONE of these is NOT one of those five principles?
A. Fasting
B. Abstinence
C. Bathing
D. Walking
E. Rocking
F. Massage

161. According to Jonathan, Greek soldiers often drank a disgusting mixture of bull and goat mucus to give them courage before battles. What was this mixture called?

162. While exploring the Tiber Island, Jonathan discovers an apothecary's stall. What twig-like plant does the apothecary recommend as a treatment for asthma?

163. The young apothecary also gives Jonathan an ointment for the healing of scars, which Jonathan applies to his branded arm. What is this ointment called?

164. Which nickname for the Tiber Island frightens Nubia?

165. What cure does Lupus employ when he stings his finger on sea-urchins' spikes?

166. Floppy gives the friends some gummy resin from Chios, which Doctor Mordecai sometimes prescribes for bad breath and stomach pains. Flavia observes that we get a word meaning 'to chew' from it. What is the Chian gum called?

167. When Captain Geminus is stabbed, what does the doctor use to fill the wounds before the skin is sewn back together?

168. What Greek word does the doctor use to describe Captain Geminus's loss of memory in *The Fugitive from Corinth*?

169. It is said that if you put the juice of the plant 'aconite' on the tip of an arrow, then shoot a wolf with that arrow, the wolf will surely die. What alternative name for aconite reflects this use?

170. According to Doctor Mordecai's manual on poison, which ONE of the following poisonous plants has no known antidote?
A. Belladonna
B. Oleander
C. Hemlock
D. Yew berries

171. For what purpose would Roman people add perfume to their wine?
    A. To aid digestion
    B. To act as a laxative
    C. To sweeten the breath
    D. For a glowing skin

172. Jonathan identifies at least ten poisonous plants within a mile's radius of the Villa Limona near Surrentum. Which ONE of the following is NOT on his list?
    A. Hellebore
    B. Belladonna
    C. Oleander
    D. Arsenic
    E. Henbane

173. Mithridatium was known as the universal antidote. It was named after the king who lived in fear of being poisoned. This king successfully invented many such remedies and became immune to all poisons. His success backfired: when ordered by a Roman Emperor to commit suicide he had to use a sword as no poison had any effect on him! What was the name of the unhappy king after which mithridatium is named?

174. Which of the following is NOT an ingredient of mithridatium?
    A. Rose petals
    B. Walnuts
    C. Dried figs
    D. Rue leaves

175. In *The Sirens of Surrentum*, Locusta describes hemlock as the noblest and gentlest of all poisons. Which famous Greek philosopher killed himself with a draft of hemlock?

176. According to Locusta, Nero's mother Agrippina killed her husband Claudius not with a poisoned fig, but with a poisoned ....

177. Taking an antidote is not always a matter of drinking a small vial of liquid and feeling instantly better. Sometimes the methods of counteracting poison are very unpleasant. Which ONE of the following methods is NOT mentioned in *The Sirens of Surrentum*?
A. Making yourself vomit
B. Forcing yourself to keep moving
C. Rolling naked in the snow
D. Drinking charcoal powder mixed in castor oil
E. Taking an enema to force a poo
F. Having your naked body rubbed all over

178. In *The Sirens of Surrentum*, which ONE of the following is NOT mentioned as a method of suicide?
A. Opening your veins (i.e. cutting your wrists)
B. Swallowing burning coals
C. Dashing your head against a wall
D. Drinking poison
E. Stabbing yourself

179. According to Flavia, most poisons were originally love-potions. From which goddess do we therefore get the word 'venom'?

180. The cure for colic in horses is a vinegar and caper-bush drench. What is a drench?

For the answers to these questions, turn to page 139.

THE COLOSSUS OF RHODES

Jason gets the *Golden Fleece*.
(Illustration based on a red-figure vase of c.350 BC)

181. With the start of the sailing season now due, Lupus wants to fulfil his uncle's dying wish to save the freeborn children who had been kidnapped and illegally sold as slaves. Who kidnapped the children?

182. What is the nationality of the ship that sets sail from Ostia without authorisation the day before the *Delphina* is due to depart?

183. Because the omens are not perfect, Captain Geminus is hesitant to set sail. In the end Lupus insists. What gives Lupus the right to demand that the *Delphina* set sail immediately?

184. The *Delphina* has two paying passengers. One is Marcus Artorius Bato, Ostia's junior magistrate. The other is a young aristocrat named Flaccus to whom Flavia takes an instant dislike. What is his gentilicium (middle name)?

185. Flavia gives Flaccus the nickname Floppy. Which ONE of the following is NOT a meaning of the Latin word 'flaccus'?
A. Floppy
B. Flabby
C. Big-eared
D. Muscular

186. Before the *Delphina* set sail, Lupus spread out the white mainsail and painted a black dolphin on it. What detail did Tigris seem to add when accidentally he ran across the sail and trod in the wet paint?

187. Flavia says translating a Greek passage is like solving a mystery. Even the smallest letters cannot be ignored, they are important clues. She names the smallest letter in the Greek alphabet as an example. Which letter is this?

188. What unusual cargo does the Rhodian crew-member Zosimus take with him on board the *Delphina*?

189. What is the name of the *Delphina*'s stowaway, who emerges on the first day of sailing?

190. Floppy's beautiful slave-boy has the same name as one of Jason's Argonauts, a young man who could fly. What is his name?

191. Inspired by the fact that Floppy has a slave with the same name as one of Jason's Argonauts, the four friends match crewmembers and passengers on the *Delphina* with the mythical characters on the *Argo*. Who gets to be Jason, the leader?

192. Who do the friends cast in the role of Acastus, the arrogant son of King Pelias?

193. Which ONE of the following is NOT part of the *Delphina*'s cargo as she sets sail from Ostia?
A. Bags of salt
B. Amphoras of fish-sauce
C. Sacks of grain
D. Crates of glassware

194. As the *Delphina* nears Sicily, the voyagers encounter a patch of warm bubbling sulphur water, a phenomenon which still occurs today. In antiquity this strange phenomenon probably gave rise to the myth of the dangerous whirlpool often linked with the sea-monster Scylla. What was the name of the mythical whirlpool?

195. Floppy and his slave-boy sniff pieces of what fruit to ward off sea-sickness?

196. Gaius Valerius Flaccus, also known as Floppy, did not write the poem about Ithaca; a modern Greek poet called Cavafy did. However, we do have part of a poem by Flaccus. It was an epic poem about the voyage of Jason. What was it called?

197. As the friends sail on their quest while reading the account of Jason and his Argonauts, they learn that the ship which took the kidnapped children has an appropriately ominous name. What is the ship's name?

198. Many rumours are circulated about the mastermind who runs the illegal slave trade. Which ONE of the following is NOT mentioned in this story?
A. That he is a child
B. That he is a woman
C. That he is a giant
D. That he is mute

199. Valerius Flaccus and Apollonius Rhodius were not the only ancient poets to compose a version of the Argonautica. After leaving Corinth, Flavia and her friends abandon Apollonius' Greek original and pick up a Latin translation. What was the name of the translator?
A. Catullus
B. Varro
C. Horace
D. Virgil

200. Which ONE of the following is NOT mentioned as being a product of Rhodes?
A. Fighting cockerels
B. Rose-scented perfume
C. Novelty oil-flasks
D. Falernian wine
E. Rock-hard biscuits called 'hardbake'

201. Lupus visits a rocky island and meets an exiled Roman matron and her Jewish slave-boy. At one point Lupus lights a signal fire in a cave. Little does he know that not many years later, St John the Evangelist will have Revelations in that very cave. What is the name of this island of exile?

202. Which ONE of the following disasters does NOT befall the four detectives on their journey to Rhodes?
A. Falling yard-arm
B. Galley fire
C. Killer whale

D. Sulphurous whirlpool

E. Sudden storm

203. The first relative Lupus meets on Symi is his ancient, tiny, withered great-grandmother. What is her name?

204. After the storm abates, the *Delphina* takes refuge in a sheltered harbour beneath a town made of coloured marble, 'the most beautiful city' Nubia has ever seen. In antiquity this town was famous for a nude statue of Aphrodite, which was almost as famous as the Seven Wonders. What is the name of this port town?

205. When the friends sail into Rhodes, they see dozens of enormous statues silhouetted on the skyline. Why can't they see the Colossus of Rhodes?

206. The Colossus of Rhodes was a giant statue of Helios the sun god. It inspired Nero's colossal statue in Rome and the modern Statue of Liberty. What did the spikes on the Colossus' crown represent?

207. Because of a plague of snakes on the island of Rhodes, the men there never wear sandals but only ....

208. On what street in Rhodes Town does Magnus live?

A. Street of the Silversmiths

B. Street of the Coppersmiths
C. Street of the Glassblowers
D. Street of the Ironmongers

209. In the sanctuary of Apollo on Rhodes, Lupus remembers a prayer he made at the amphitheatre in Rome. Lupus had prayed to Jonathan's god, vowing that if he would save Jonathan, Lupus would give something in return. What did Lupus vow to give to God?

210. Which ONE of the following is NOT part of the *Delphina*'s cargo as she sets sail from Rhodes?
A. Corinthian bronzes
B. Sponges from Symi
C. Rose-scented oil
D. Marble blocks from Cnidos
E. Mastic-flavoured hardbakex
F. Calymnian honey

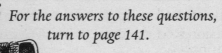

For the answers to these questions, turn to page 141.

TRAVEL AND TRANSPORT

211. The Mediterranean Sea was the centre of the Roman World. Ancient Romans called it 'mare nostrum'. What does that mean?

212. The 'mare inferum' is the Roman name for the sea near Ostia, where Flavia and her friends often paddle. In the Roman Mysteries, what is this part of the Mediterranean called?

213. The quickest and easiest way of transporting products around the Roman Empire was by ship. The most important cargo by far was the grain from Egypt and North Africa which fed Rome's million inhabitants. In Flavia's time the huge grain ships docked in Portus, the new harbour of Ostia, just north of the River Tiber. Which Emperor built Portus?

214. Private merchant ships often dealt in luxury goods. Which ONE of the following would NOT have been transported in first century Roman times?
    A. Wine from Campania
    B. Slaves from Judaea
    C. Wild beasts from Mauretania
    D. Vanilla from Yucatan

E. Ivory from Africa

F. Garum from Hispania

G. Olive-oil from Massilia

H. Glassware from Alexandria

215. According to Flavia's old nursemaid Alma, what is even more dangerous than mad dogs, volcanoes, assassins, plague, fire and wild-beasts?

216. Despite the hazards of sea travel, a few Romans were rich and brave enough to travel simply for enjoyment and education. These ancient tourists often visited the 'Seven Sights'. What do we call the 'Seven Sights' today?

217. Roman sailors were extremely superstitious. Which ONE of the following actions does Captain Geminus NOT claim will incur bad luck on a sea voyage?
A. Setting sail on Thursday
B. Setting sail on an odd day of the month
C. Stepping onto the ship with left foot first
D. Sneezing on board ship
E. Dreaming of owls or bears the night before setting sail

218. Which 'L' word was the purification ceremony for a ship, often involving the sacrifice of a vastly expensive animal like a bull?

219. As he stands on a pier of Ostia's smaller harbour – south of the River Tiber – Aristo looks north and pronounces that 'the wind is perfect'. How can he tell which direction the wind is blowing?

220. Who does Captain Geminus have to check in with every time he enters or leaves a port?

221. Like many Roman merchant ships, the *Delphina* has a carved wooden swan's neck ornament looking back towards a small skiff which is usually towed behind. What is the name of the *Delphina's* skiff?

222. When Flavia and her friends first sail out of Ostia's harbour in April of AD 80, the skiff tows the *Delphina*, not the other way around. Here is a list of situations in which the skiff might have to tow the mother ship. Which of the following is the least likely of these?
    A. If there is not enough wind close to shore
    B. If there is wind, but the harbour entrance is too narrow to enter or exit under sail
    C. If the ship has been damaged in some way
    D. If the ship is passing between clashing rocks

223. In order to steer the ship, the captain or helmsman would hold a polished wooden rod attached to two steering paddles. What do we call the rod that controls the direction of a ship?

224. As the *Delphina* sails away from Ostia, her passengers cluster on a platform at the back of the ship to wave goodbye to friends and family. What do we call the back of a ship?

225. On the second day out of Ostia sailing south, the *Delphina* passes an island near the Bay of Naples, said to be the home of the Sirens. Some poets called this island Anthemoessa. Most Romans called it Caprea. What do we call it today?

226. Sailors in Roman times always liked to keep land in sight, but sometimes they had to cross open sea. Without landmarks, how could they tell where they were going?

227. Captain Geminus decides to head for the Greek islands via the Isthmus of Corinth rather than the notorious cape at the southern end of mainland Greece. What was the name of this dreaded cape?

228. Although Nero began to cut a canal through the Isthmus of Corinth, in the late first century AD it was not completed. Ships had to be placed on rollers and pulled along a kind of track. What was this track called?

229. The ancient Greeks and Romans had names for all the winds. What is the name of the warm westerly breeze which fills the sails as the *Delphina* leaves Corinth's eastern port in *The Colossus of Rhodes*?
    A. Auster
    B. Boreas
    C. Aquilo
    D. Zephyrus

230. Passengers on most merchant ships had to provide their own food and a slave to prepare it. What is special about mealtimes on the *Delphina*?

231. Which ONE of the following was NOT a part of the *Delphina*'s rigging?
    A. Forestays
    B. Halyards
    C. Abafts
    D. Lifts
    E. Brails

232. A small slanting foremast and sail began to appear on Roman ships in the first century AD. What is the name of the sail which hangs from this slanting foremast?
    A. The artemon
    B. The blizzen
    C. The mizzen
    D. The temenos
    E. Tenedos

233. One of the best accounts of a shipwreck from Roman times is found in the New Testament in the twenty-seventh chapter of Acts. After a storm which lasted over two weeks, a big grain ship from Alexandra finally broke up on the shore of Malta. Miraculously, all 276 passengers survived. Who was its most famous survivor?

234. If a sailor survived a shipwreck he would cut off something and offer it as thanks in a temple of Neptune. What would the survivor dedicate?

235. The horse played a fairly unimportant role in Roman transportation. Oxen were used for heavy loads. The most popular beast of transport for light and medium loads was a hybrid of horse and donkey. What was this animal?

236. One important type of long-distance traveller would use a succession of fast horses. Which one?
A. The Emperor
B. An imperial messenger
C. A Vestal Virgin
D. A travel writer

237. Maps and guide books existed in Roman times, though few have survived. In *The Fugitive from Corinth*, Jonathan acquires a guidebook of Corinth in codex form. Which ONE of the following is NOT true of his guidebook?
A. It is made of papyrus pages
B. It uses the three colour printing method
C. It is the size and shape of a wax tablet
D. It rates hotels, inns and taverns
E. It describes noteworthy landmarks

238. Despite the rating system for inns and taverns, many were terrible fleapits, with inedible food and unsanitary conditions. None were as bad as the one from the story of Theseus, however, with its bed of torture. What was the innkeeper's name?

239. Tour guides were known in ancient times, ready to pounce on the innocent tourist, just like today.

When Flavia and her friends arrive in Delphi, a cheerful young guide with the appearance of a laughing faun attaches himself to them. His name means someone who 'leads people into mysteries' in Greek. What is his name?

240. Shop-keepers and souvenir sellers accosted tourists in Roman times, too. When Flavia and her friends arrive in the Roman-looking market outside the sanctuary of Apollo at Delphi, they are offered many things in exchange for their money. Which ONE of the following is NOT one of them?
A. Hot sausages
B. Apollo ashtrays
C. Dream garlands
D. Guidebooks, maps and descriptions of the monuments
E. Comedies and Tragedies

For the answers to these questions, turn to page 142.

THE FUGITIVE FROM CORINTH

Orestus pursued by Furies.
(Illustration based on a red-figure vase of c.380 BC)

241. What is the name of the young Greek who saved Captain Geminus's life when he was attacked in a Corinthian tavern?

242. According to the Greek geographer and travel writer Pausanias, the names of Corinth's two ports came from Leches and Cenchrias, said to be the children of Poseidon. What did the Romans call Poseidon?

243. Rome destroyed the Greek city of Corinth in 146 BC. Later, most of Greece became a Roman province called Achaea. What city became the capital of this province?

244. Although Flavia and her friends are due to set sail from Lechaeum, Corinth's western port, they are spending the night in a luxury hotel near Cenchrea, the eastern port of Corinth. One of the reasons is that Helen, the owner of the hotel, is a friend of Flavia's father. What 'H' word was Latin for a luxury hotel?

245. The first doctor who treats Captain Geminus does several things which make Jonathan doubt his ability. Which ONE of the following does NOT cause Jonathan unease?
A. He considers bleeding him
B. He doesn't wash his hands first
C. He asks for oil and vinegar
D. He insensitively asks the captain's own daughter to clean the wounds
E. He can't seem to thread a needle

246. When Jonathan searches the hotel for clues, he finds a souvenir Flavia had brought her father from Rome – a folding knife with an iron blade and bronze handle. What is the handle shaped like?

247. When Captain Geminus regains consciousness, he asks for his wife who has been dead for eight years. What was her name?

248. To help the detectives in their quest, Helen gives them a carruca and four mules. She has named each mule after a spice. Which spice is Piper named after?

249. Jonathan's guidebook tells all about Theseus, the hero who grew up near Corinth, then sailed to Crete to kill the Minotaur. The Minotaur was a mythical monster, half man and half ....?

250 Before sailing to Crete, Theseus had other adventures. To discover his birthright he first had to be strong enough to lift an enormous rock hiding his father's sword and sandals. What was his father's name?

251. When Theseus set out to claim his birthright as King of Athens, he travelled via the Isthmus of Corinth. Along the way he subdued brigands and monsters. One of the criminals he punished was a man who tied people to pine trees bent down from either side of the road, then let go of the trees, thus causing his unfortunate victim to be torn in two. What was the brigand's name?

252. When the friends arrive at the Diolkos Tavern, Jonathan notices their room smells awful, probably because nobody's 'emptied the vespasian for days'. What does Jonathan mean by 'vespasian'.

253. Today, if you travel from Corinth to Athens along the old coast road you soon begin to ascend steep cliffs. Local Greeks call this place 'kaka skala' which is exactly what it was known as in ancient times. Knowing the story of Theseus and Sciron, you might be able to guess what 'kaka skala' means?

254. Pausanias saw 'Sciron's Rock' in the sea below the cliffs and you can still see it today. Sciron was a robber who forced travellers to stop and wash his feet. When they had finished he would kick them over the cliff to his man-eating pet. What kind of animal was Sciron's pet?

255. On the road to Athens the travellers look out over the Saronic Gulf towards the island of Salamis, the site of a great Athenian victory. Which empire's fleet was defeated at the battle of Salamis?

256. The Furies were mythical creatures who pursued those who had committed particularly terrible crimes and drove them mad. Which of these is not a name used to refer to them?
A. The Kindly Ones
B. The Ones Who Must Not Be Named
C. Eumenides
D. The Scylla

257. According to Flavia, which ONE of the following does NOT describe the mythical Furies?
A. They carry torches
B. They fire poisoned arrows
C. They crack whips
D. They have red eyes
E. They have black tongues
F. They have snaky hair

258. In Greek mythology and literature, a young man named Orestes was pursued by the Furies after Apollo told him to murder his mother. What was the name of Orestes' mother?

259. When Orestes was pursued by the Furies, where did he go to seek sanctuary?

260. According to Atticus, which is the biggest and most important town of mainland Greece?
   A. Athens
   B. Thebes
   C. Corinth
   D. Delphi

261. Thebes is the capital of a region of Greece called Boeotia. According to Atticus, what does Boeotia mean?

262. After a prophecy that baby Oedipus will do terrible things, his parents expose him on a hillside. A shepherd finds the baby and gives him to the King and Queen of which Greek town?

263. According to Jonathan's guidebook, what is the name of the famous crossroads where Oedipus unknowingly killed his own father?

264. The prophetess at Delphi was named after a big snake called Python, which lived in a cave. What was the Delphic prophetess called?

265. When the friends arrive in Delphi, they need a place to stay. Jonathan's guidebook recommends a high-quality hospitium near a spring where murderers can cleanse themselves of pollution. What is the name of Delphi's famous purifying spring?

266. Which word beginning with 'T' means the sacred boundary of a precinct?

267. As the friends near Athens for the second time, they approach the sanctuary of Demeter at Eleusis, famous for its mysterious rites and rituals. According to Jonathan's guidebook, what is the punishment for people who enter the sanctuary without permission?

268. In Athens, Flavia and her friends explore the agora. Here they see groups of men strolling in the shade of a long stoa with painted columns. The men dress differently, to show who they are. Which ONE of the following groups do the friends NOT see in the agora of Athens?
    A. Pythagoreans, with long hair and short brown capes
    B. Epicureans, clean-shaven and with short hair
    C. Cynics, with long matted beards
    D. Athletes, wearing no clothes at all
    E. Priests of Isis, bald and with long white robes

269. Which ONE of the following do Flavia and Nubia NOT see when they enter the Parthenon, the great temple to Athena?
    A. A colossal bronze statue of Athena
    B. A reflecting pool before the statue
    C. Translucent white roof tiles overhead
    D. Masses of treasure behind bronze grilles
    E. An upper balcony where people can walk

270. The friends have a meal at the Hydria Tavern near the Tower of the Winds in the Roman Agora. One dish they have is so delicious that Flavia calls it

ambrosia. Which ONE of the following ingredients does NOT appear in Flavia's 'ambrosia'?

A. Yoghurt
B. Dill weed
C. Garlic
D. Potato
E. Cucumber

For the answers to these questions, turn to page 143.

THE ILLUSTRATED ARISTO'S SCROLL

At the back of each of the Roman Mysteries is a glossary of unfamiliar words, with definitions. Have you ever wondered what these people, places and objects really looked like? Here are pictures of fifteen objects, all of which you'll find in Aristo's scrolls. For each picture on pages 76-77, can you find its name and description? The answers are on page 144.

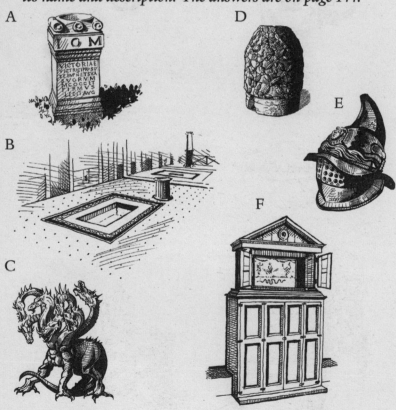

A

B

C

D

E

F

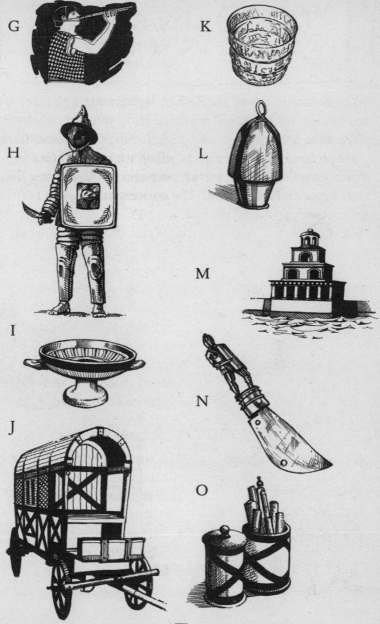

G

K

H

L

M

I

N

J

O

271. Altar	1. An elegant, Greek, flat-bowled drinking cup, especially for dinner parties.
272. Aulos	2. A lighthouse.
273. Bleeding cup	3. A flat-topped, stone block used for making an offering to a god or goddess.
274. Capsa	4. Metal shin-guards worn by a gladiator.
275. Carruca	5. A stone altar at Delphi which represented the centre of the world.
276. Chariot beaker	6. A vessel made of glass used to commemorate events at the Circus Maximus.
277. Gladiator's knife	7. A four-wheeled travelling carriage, usually mule-driven and often covered.
278. Greaves	8. The many-headed serpent which Heracles valiantly fought.

279. Hydra	9. A rectangular rainwater pool, under a skylight, located in the atrium.
280. Impluvium	10. A household shrine, often a chest with a miniature temple on top.
281. Kylix	11. Part of a gladiator's armour.
282. Lararium	12. A weapon used by a gladiator.
283. Murmillo's helmet	13. Vessel used as a means of releasing poison from the body via the veins.
284. Omphalos	14. A cylindrical leather case, usually for medical implements.
285. Pharus	15. A wind instrument with double pipes and reeds that makes a buzzy sound.

THE SIRENS OF SURRENTUM

Lashed to the mast of his ship,
Odysseus listens to the Sirens' song.
(Illustration based on a red-figure vase of c.490 BC)

286. Pulchra – the beautiful daughter of Pollius Felix –
has invited Flavia and her friends to Surrentum.
She has asked them to bring books on which
subject?

287. Flavia has been reading Virgil's *Aeneid* and
thinking about love and destiny. For example, the
Trojan hero Aeneas had to abandon Queen Dido
because he was destined to marry a beautiful
Italian princess. What was the name of the
princess?

288. Captain Geminus forbids his daughter to
visit a notorious town on the Bay of Naples
because it is a 'glirarium of licentiousness'. What
is a glirarium?

289. What is the name of Pulchra's puppy?

290. Felix's wife, Polla Argentaria, likes the local
wine, called Surrentinum. But Felix describes it
as tasting like:
A. Honeyed posca
B. Mule's pee
C. Noble vinegar
D. Weak poison

291. Three young widows and three eligible bachelors
have been invited to the Villa Limona. What is the
name of the beautiful, black-haired widow who
arrives in a litter carried by four Ethiopians and
who has a black panther on a lead?

292. One of the three eligible bachelors used to live in a villa near Herculaneum which was buried by Vesuvius. His magnificent villa had a famous library with over 1,800 papyrus scrolls on Greek and Roman philosophy. Today we know this house as the 'Villa of the Papyri'. According to *The Sirens of Surrentum*, what was the name of its young owner?
   A. Lucilius
   B. Flaccus
   C. Vopiscus
   D. Philodemus

293. The Sirens were mythical creatures – half women, half bird – who played music on rocks and lured sailors to their deaths. Several of the Villa Limona slave-girls are named after Sirens. Which one of the following is NOT the name of a Siren?
   A. Calypso
   B. Parthenope
   C. Leucosia
   D. Ligea

294. Flavia celebrates her eleventh birthday in this story. Which ONE of the following gifts is her present from Pulchra?
   A. Portraits of the four friends
   B. An ebony hairpin
   C. A scroll of Seneca's letters
   D. A make-up kit
   E. A glass signet ring of Minerva

295. Pulchra has invited a boy called Tranquillus to the house-party at the Villa Limona. Young Tranquillus has already compiled a book of Greek swear words, but expresses a desire to be a biographer when he grows up. He does indeed grow up to be a famous Roman biographer. Today we know him better by his gentilicium (middle name). What is this?

296. Romans loved to eat small birds. A common way of catching them was to smear long flexible rods with a yellow, sticky substance and then raise the sticks into the branches. When birds land on the sticky rods they cannot fly away. The sticky substance was made of mashed mistletoe berries. What was it called?

297. What is the Latin word for a 'home-grown' slave, i.e. one born of slave parents or of a slave-girl and her master?

298. What is the Epicurean concept of *ataraxia*?
    A. The state of being consumed by love
    B. Freedom from passion
    C. Not having to pay taxes to the Emperor
    D. Total submission to pleasure

299. Flavia has been reading lots of Latin love poets. Which ONE of the following is NOT among them?
    A. Propertius
    B. Ovid
    C. Catullus

D. Virgil

E. Sappho

300. During her stay at the Villa Limona, Nubia sees a beautiful horse called Pegasus, with very unusual colouring. Pegasus has a dark brown coat, but what colour are his mane and tail?

301. As her birthday treat, Flavia is allowed to join the adults for the *secunda mensa* of their banquet. What would we call *secunda mensa* today?

302. While at the grown-ups' dinner party, Flavia is asked to identify the mythical scene on an oenochoe (wine jug) of great antiquity. Which Greek hero is shown on it?

303. One of the young widows, Annia Serena, has an unusually acute sense of smell and can tell one perfume from another. Which ONE of the following is NOT an expensive perfume mentioned in this story?
   A. Ambrosium – made of vanilla, eucalyptus, hibiscus and musk
   B. Metopium – made of cardamom, balsam, honey and bitter almond
   C. Susinum – made of rose, myrrh, cinnamon and saffron
   D. Saffron – pure essence of the crocus stamen and 'number one' oil at the Baths of Nero

304. According to Tranquillus, what was the name of the Emperor Nero's famous poisoner?

305. In a cockfight at the Villa Limona, the furious birds are not released until the command is given. What Latin imperative does Felix's slave Justus give to make them fight?

306. Fifteen years before this story takes place, Nero committed the terrible crime of matricide when he ordered the assassination of his own mother, who was staying at her villa on the Bay of Naples. What was the name of Nero's mother?

307. Shortly after Nero had his mother killed, upper-class Romans plotted to depose him. But their conspiracy was uncovered and many of them were ordered to commit suicide. One of these was Polla Argentaria's first husband, a young and promising poet. What was his name?

308. Another of the Romans who was implicated in the conspiracy against Nero was Nero's old tutor, who had become a famous philosopher and writer. What was his name?

309. What type of food was the Lucrine Lake famous for producing in Roman times?

310. Polla advises Flavia to marry a man of *arête*. How does she define the Greek word *arête*?

311. Stoics are said to be indifferent to passion and always seek the *summum bonum* – the highest good – which consists of four principles. Which ONE of the following is NOT one of these four principles?
    A. Wisdom
    B. Self-control
    C. Charity
    D. Justice
    E. Courage

312. Polla Argentaria quotes Seneca's story of a brave barbarian from Germania who decided to kill himself rather than die in the arena as entertainment for his hated captors. What did the barbarian use to choke himself?

313. The famous philosopher Seneca wrote many letters of advice to a young Roman. What was his friend's name?
    A. Lucilius
    B. Flaccus

C. Vopiscus
D. Philodemus

314. Flavia leaves bait to trap the poisoner at a small shrine to Aphrodite Sosandra, the 'Venus Who Saves Men'. What is noteworthy about the statue of Aphrodite in this shrine?

315. All of the following aspects of Flavia's behaviour outraged Tranquillus's father, except one. Which one?

A. She went into an olive grove with his son
B. She was seen holding his son's hand
C. She kissed his son in public
D. She was barefoot at the time
E. Her hair was unpinned at the time

For the answers to these questions, turn to page 144.

QUIPS AND QUOTATIONS

316. Complete this saying: 'When a Prometheus opens a ...., Rome will be devastated.'

317. Complete this line from Aeschylus's play *Agamemnon*: 'While we sleep, the pain we can't forget falls drop by drop upon our .... '

318. What Latin expression that Alma quotes is often translated as 'Remember one day we will die'?

319. On a Roman tomb, the letters 'DM' mean 'to the spirits of the underworld'. What Latin phrase does DM stand for?

320. Inscribed on the great Temple of Apollo at Delphi is the Greek phrase *gnothi seauton*. What does it mean?

321. As Polla gazes across the Bay of Naples, she quotes Virgil: 'One moment we are fruitful and calm, the next disaster strikes. Events have tears and thoughts of death touch the soul.' What recent event is she thinking of?

322. According to the philosopher Seneca, 'Wherever you look you can find an end to your troubles.' What does Seneca mean when he says 'an end'?

323. In *The Gladiators from Capua*, when Nubia descends from the top of the amphitheatre, Sisyphus exclaims 'Nubia ex machina!' meaning 'Nubia lowered from a crane.' What famous expression – meaning 'a god from a crane' – has he adapted?

324. Flavia uses the term 'sub rosa' to mean secretly or 'in confidence'. What does it literally mean?

325. Polla Argentaria describes the two main philosophical schools: the Stoics and the Epicureans. How does she translate the Epicurean maxim: *Otium versus negotium?*

326. Who wrote that 'Pegasus glides above the clouds and under the stars, with the sky his earth, and wings instead of feet'?

327. According to Mordecai 'Most doctors think they're one step down from ....'

328. Egnatius warns Lupus: 'Never eat ....'

329. In *The Enemies of Jupiter*, who is always saying, 'I humbly bow'?

330. To Romans, the caw of the raven sounds like 'Cras! Cras!' What does this mean?

331. Finish this quote by the poet Martial, who was an eyewitness of the inaugural games in the new Flavian amphitheatre. 'Where once was water is now ....'

332. In *The Colossus of Rhodes*, Flavia explains that the word 'nauseous' comes from the Greek word *naus*. What does *naus* mean?

333. 'You know what they say about food in Greece,' says the Athenian Atticus in *The Fugitive from Corinth*, '.............., and then more ....'

334. Nubia is surprised to learn that the Greeks have a special word for someone who kills his brother. What is this word?

335. All Lupus remembers of his mother are the words of a lullaby she used to sing: 'When you come home, when you come home to ....'

336. When an eastern king once asked the Delphic oracle if he should attack his enemy, she famously replied, 'If you cross a certain river, a great kingdom will be destroyed.' The king duly crossed the river to attack his enemy, but his own kingdom was destroyed! In *The Enemies of Jupiter*, Flavia mistakenly identifies this king as Xerxes. In *The Fugitive from Corinth*, Jonathan corrects her, telling her it was a king of Lydia, not Persia. What was his name?

337. Flavia consults the Delphic oracle and – as usual – the reply is cryptic. In Greek hexameter, the Pythia promises that Flavia's father 'will regain his reason on the day it rains from a clear sky.' What does Flavia later do to unwittingly fulfil this prophecy?

338. Complete this quote of Ovid: 'A loose-netted
.... that breaks free is not good.'

339. When Flavia joins an adult dinner-party in *The
Sirens of Surrentum*, she is expected to provide a
literary quote, so she recites the first lines of a
Greek epic poem. Which one?

340. When Flavia is searching Felix's bedroom for clues,
she finds a poem on his desk, and her eye catches
one particular phrase in Greek. '.................. on
their rocks.' What is the missing word?

341. According to Polla Argentaria, the poet Propertius
begged his girlfriend to 'depart from corrupt
.................., whose shores are dangerous to
virtuous girls.'

342. Flavia thinks of Felix when she quotes this passage
of Virgil. Can you fill in the blank? 'Aeneas
stepped forward, brilliant in the clear light, with
the face and shoulders of a ....'

343. Arria and Paetus were commanded to commit
suicide when it was discovered that they were
involved in a plot to assassinate the Emperor
Claudius. Arria plunged the dagger into her
breast, removed it and handed it to her fearful
husband with the famous words: 'It does not
..................'

344. Having gleaned some useful information from the tipsy grooms of the Villa Limona, Tranquillus quotes the famous Latin motto 'in vino veritas', meaning 'In wine there is ....'

345. At the midsummer's eve beach banquet, Felix quotes Virgil. Can you supply the missing word? .... is near and he would say: 'I'm coming soon so live today.'

For the answers to these questions, turn to page 145.

MYTHS AND LEGENDS

346. According to the myth, a beautiful woman once boasted that she was more beautiful than Venus. Her hubris was punished. She became the most hideous creature ever seen, so ugly that her looks turned people to stone. What was her name?

347. A Titan called Prometheus displeased Jupiter by bringing something to man. What?

348. As punishment, Jupiter chained the immortal Prometheus to a rock and sent a vulture to torment him. What does the vulture do to Prometheus, who can't die?

349. Pandora's box contained fear, hatred, disease and death – and one last thing trapped inside. What is it?

350. In the Temple of Apollo on the Palatine Hill, Ascletario shows Flavia and her friends the cult statue of Apollo and his sister and his mother. Apollo's sister was Diana. What was the name of Apollo's mother?

351. The mother of Castor and Pollux, and also of Helen and Clytemnestra had a name similar to that of Apollo's mother. What was it?

352. Aesculapius is often shown with a staff and with his special animal. What is this animal?

353. As punishment for his hubris, Aesculapius was killed by Jupiter. What did Jupiter use to kill him?

354. Which of the following mythical monsters is NOT connected to Theseus:
    A. The man-eating turtle
    B. The man-eating horse
    C. The man-eating sow
    D. The minotaur

355. In mythology, who took the form of an eagle to kidnap a beautiful boy called Ganymede?

356. Which tragic Greek hero murdered his father, married his mother and then put out his own eyes?

357. Which ONE of the following was NOT one of the 'monsters' encountered by Jason on his quest for the Golden Fleece?
A. The Cyclops
B. The Sirens
C. Scylla
D. The Harpies

358. What is the name of Odysseus' home island, and also of a famous poem by Constantine Cavafy which is paraphrased in *The Colossus of Rhodes*?

359. In *The Sirens of Surrentum*, Polla Argentaria likens herself to a tragic character from Virgil's *Aeneid*. What is the name of the character?

360. Seneca's advice to a young friend was to 'stop up your ears with something stronger than wax'. In mythology, who stopped up his sailors' ears with wax, but left his own unplugged, so that he could clearly hear the Siren's song?

361. On the obverse of a silver denarius in *The Charioteer of Delphi* is the emperor's brother, Domitian. What mythical creature is shown on the reverse of this coin?

362. According to Flavia, the mythical flying horse called Pegasus was born of Medusa. Who was Pegasus' father?

363. When Pegasus was fully grown, a hero named Bellerophon tamed him with a magic bridle. Who gave Bellerophon the bridle?

364. The chimera was the monster Bellerophon defeated with Pegasus's help. Which of the following does not describe the chimera?
A. Head of a lion
B. Tail of a snake
C. Body of a goat
D. Eyes of a wolf

365. What affliction befell King David's enemies when they captured the Ark of the Covenant?

366. Which lyre-strumming hero from Greek mythology journeyed to the underworld to bring back his dead wife Euridyce?

367. What is the title given to Apollonius Rhodius's poem about Jason's search for the golden fleece?

368. In Apollonius's version of the quest for the Golden Fleece, Jason encounters a walking bronze giant on the island of Crete and must disable it by pulling a plug in its heel to release its life substance or ichor. What is the name of the bronze giant?

369. The Roman poet Martial wrote this poem about a dwarf: 'If you saw just his head, you'd believe he was Hector, but if you saw him standing up,

you'd think he was Astyanax.' Hector was the great Trojan hero of Homer's *Iliad*. Who was Astyanax?

370. A phenomenon now known as St Elmo's Fire manifests itself on board the *Delphina* at the end of a storm. The sailors on board the *Delphina* believe that the two eerie blue 'flames' at either end of the yardarm represent the heavenly twins. Who are these twins?

371. At the upstream end of the Tiber Island was a secluded sacred precinct to a god who was half goat, half man; Faunus. What other name do we know him by?

372. According to Pliny the Elder, the island of Rhodes suffered a plague of snakes. The Rhodians sent envoys to the oracle at Delphi who told them to import a certain kind of animal. These animals, said the Pythia, would suck all the snakes from their holes and devour them, thus ending the plague. This plan worked, and the imported animal is now the symbol of Rhodes. What is it?

373. The streets of Rhodes Town are like a maze and Flavia says they need a thread to help them find their way out again. Which mythical princess gave Theseus a thread to help him find his way back out of the labyrinth?

374. Flavia decides to offer a votive to the gods along with her prayers for Scopas's recovery. She finally buys a little bronze sculpture shaped like a centaur. A centaur was half man, half what?

For the answers to these questions, turn to page 147.

THE CHARIOTEER OF DELPHI

Pegasus the flying horse.
(Illustration based on a fragment of a red-figure vase)

375. A Greek youth named Scopas arrives from Delphi at the start of the book. Among other things, he wants Flavia and her friends to help him gain employment with one of the chariot-racing factions in Rome. Who prophesied that Scopas would be a successful charioteer?

376. In a previous adventure, Flavia and her friends rescue a baker's son. This boy is a keen fan of chariot-racing, and he helps them find a position for Scopas. What is his name?

377. All four chariot-racing factions in Rome have stables in the Field of Mars. What is the Latin term for 'Field of Mars', which Flavia and her friends use?

378. Nubia celebrates her twelfth birthday at the beginning of this book. Her three friends have chipped together to buy her a rather expensive present. What?

379. There are several strange aspects of Scopas's behaviour. Which ONE of the following is NOT one of them?
   A. He stands very stiffly
   B. He keeps his cloak on, even though it is a hot day
   C. He speaks in a loud, flat voice
   D. He has a nervous tic: his eye twitches
   E. He sometimes refers to himself as 'Scopas'

380. Scopas is autistic, and like some autistic people he experiences 'synaesthesia' where the brain associates colours, smells and tastes with numbers and emotions. Which colour does Scopas associate with being 'unwell'?

381. Occasionally Scopas mutters a strange phrase under his breath. Can you remember what it is?

382. The friends receive a message from Scopas on a piece of papyrus, although he cannot read or write. Who wrote the message?

383. Knowing that Flavia and her friends are good at solving mysteries, Scopas has written to tell them about the reward offered for a missing racehorse. How much is the reward?

384. Nubia has been having vivid dreams of a beautiful stallion called Pegasus whom she saw at the Villa Limona earlier that summer. What did Pegasus refuse to do while Felix was riding him?

385. The vigiles patrolled Rome and Ostia, always on the lookout against crime and fire. Which ONE of the following things did they NOT wear or carry?
A. Canvas hoses to direct flow of water from fountain
B. Woven mats to smother fires
C. Leather buckets which could be filled with water
D. Hobnailed boots

386. When Flavia and her friends arrive in Rome to search for the missing racehorse, they stay with Flavia's aunt and uncle. Senator Cornix's Greek secretary is delighted to see them, as usual. What is his name?

387. Which ONE of the following souvenirs do the friends NOT see for sale at stalls near the stables of the chariot-racing factions?
A. Models of chariots
B. Scythian ponies
C. Miniature whips
D. Skullcaps in the colours of the four factions
E. Clay oil-lamps with images of chariots on them

388. When Jonathan sees the inscription FACTIO PRASINA above the door of a large building in the Campus Martius he knows he has found what?

389. Incitatus – Caligula's favourite stallion – had an elaborately decorated stall which by Flavia's time was used to house sick horses. Which ONE of the following was NOT among its original features?
A. Golden water trough
B. Silver gate
C. Ivory manger
D. Silken couch
E. Frescoed walls

390. Counting Sagitta, there are four horses in the original alpha team of the Greens. Which of them does Lupus like best?
A. Latro, 'fast and brave'
B. Bubalo, the steady inside horse
C. Glaucus, whose dame was Greek and whose sire was Italian
D. Sagitta, the 'Captain'

391. Hippiatros is the name of the veterinarian at the Stables of the Greens. This name is very suitable because in Greek it means 'Doctor of ....'?

392. According to Urbanus, Nubia's beloved Pegasus comes from Mauretania. This is very fitting. On which continent was Roman Mauritania?
A. Africa
B. Europe
C. Asia
D. Antarctica

393. What affliction causes Aristo to abandon the friends in the middle of their search for the missing racehorse?

394. Lupus identifies Sagitta by the narrow white blaze on the horse's forehead. Flavia realises the stallion is called Sagitta because this white mark looks like a white ....

395. Which ONE of the following events did NOT occur on the day before the races, the so-called Probatio Equorum?
   A. Horses were taken to the Circus Maximus so they could get a feel for it
   B. Horses were checked by veterinarians
   C. Horses were given practice runs
   D. A horse from each faction was sacrificed to Neptune

396. At one point, Nubia gets a very close look at the meta or 'turning posts' of the hippodrome. Which ONE of the following does NOT describe them?
   A. There are three of them at each end of the central barrier
   B. They are gilded
   C. They are cone-shaped
   D. They are as tall as a cypress tree
   E. They have intricate designs on their sides

397. The central barrier of the Circus Maximus consisted of five long rectangular basins filled with water. Rising from one of the basins was a spiral pillar with a statue on top. The statue had wings sprouting from its back and carried a wreath and a palm branch. Who was he or she?

398. Many scholars call the central barrier of the Circus Maximus the 'spina' or 'backbone'. But ancient writers used another word much more frequently. They called it the 'euripus'. What does 'euripus' mean?

399. According to Urbanus, each of the four factions represents one of the four seasons of the year. Which of the four factions do you think represents winter?

400. What is the main ingredient of the special bravery potion drunk by charioteers before a race?

401. Castor tells the story of an ex-cavalry racehorse called Imperator who bolted whenever he heard a certain sound. What sound?

402. On the first and last day of the races, emperors would lead a procession, or 'pompa' into the arena. According to Suetonius, Titus used to drive in a ceremonial chariot along with a gold and ivory statue in the likeness of his boyhood friend. In whose likeness was the statue made?

403. As the charioteers of the four different factions begin to enter the hippodrome, a huge cheer goes up. For which faction are the people cheering when they scream 'Veneti!'?

404. According to Urbanus, 'Life's a Circus' and 'The Circus is a World'. Everything in the hippodrome is symbolic. Which of the following does he NOT mention?
   A. The twenty-four races represent the hours of the day
   B. The twelve lanes represent the months of the year

C. The seven laps represent the days of the week
D. The four colours represent the four seasons
E. The obelisk on the central barrier represents the sun
F. The statue of Diana on the central barrier represents the moon
G. The water in the central barrier represents the sea

For the answers to these questions, turn to page 148.

ARCHITECTURE

With thanks to contributing Quizmaster Andrew Downey

405. According to Ascletario – who is showing Flavia and her friends around the Palatine Hill – the columns of the Temple of Jupiter on the Capitoline Hill are painted in the Etruscan style. How are they painted?

406. The pediment of the Temple of Jupiter on the Capitoline Hill is also in the Etruscan style, having no scene depicted inside. What shape is the pediment of a Greek, Roman or Etruscan temple?

407. The imperial library is located in the Temple of Apollo on the Palatine Hill. Between its columns are statues of Niobe's fourteen children, shown being slaughtered by Apollo and Diana. Niobe's seven daughters are carved of red marble. Of what colour marble are her seven sons carved?

408. In Rome, what is the name of the cattle market that lies between the Circus Maximus and the River Tiber?

409. Which ONE of the following instructions would NOT help a litter-bearer identify the house of Senator Cornix in Rome?
A. On the Caelian Hill
B. At the foot of the Aqueduct Claudia
C. Sky-blue door
D. Fierce watchdog chained outside
E. Bronze door-knocker
F. Door slave named Bulbus

410. What seventy-foot high object on the Tiber Island gives the appearance of a ship's mast?

411. Nero built the Golden House to hold dinner parties. What was its function when the new Flavian amphitheatre was opened?

412. Near the Flavian amphitheatre was a fountain called the Meta Sudans. It had a distinctive geometrical shape, just like the metas in the Circus Maximus. What shape?

413. How many arches is the Trigemina Gate at the entrance to Rome made up of?

414. When the friends first see the new Flavian amphitheatre in *The Gladiators from Capua*, Flavia points out the three types of columns on it. Which ONE of the following order of columns does she NOT mention?
A. Doric
B. Tuscan

C. Ionic

D. Corinthian

415. What is the large, rectangular stone object set before most temples?

416. According to Ascletario, people with incurable diseases sleep in a special dream court at the Temple of Aesculapius. What is the name of this 'dream court'?

417. The Colossus of Rhodes was one of the Seven Wonders of the World. Flavia learns that the criminal mastermind, Magnus, comes from a town in Asia near one of the other Seven Wonders – a giant tomb to a man called Mausolus. Where is this so-called Mausoleum?

418. One of the Seven Wonders was a lighthouse. Where was this lighthouse?

419. A Temple at Ephesus was also one of the so-named Seven Wonders. To whom was this temple dedicated?

420. Which of the Seven Wonders was located in Olympia, in Greece?

421. Which of the Seven Wonders can still be seen in Giza?

422. The final Wonder was located in Mordecai's home town. Name the Wonder and its location.

423. According to Floppy, what is a common mistake people make about the position of the Colossus of Rhodes?

424. Pausanias wrote a travel guide to Greece in Roman times. Thanks to him we know which monuments were standing in Corinth, Delphi and Athens around the time of Flavia. According to Pausanias – and *The Fugitive from Corinth* – which ONE of these would you NOT associate with the entrance to Corinth?
A. A cypress grove, known as Craneum
B. A triumphal arch topped by a gilded chariot
C. A fountain dedicated to Orpheus
D. A large bronze statue of Poseidon
E. A road going down to Lechaeum

425. The colonnaded road leading from Corinth to its western port Lechaeum reminds Flavia of another covered road in Italy. A Roman poet called Statius also notes the similarities between the Corinthian covered road and the Italian one. To whose villa does the Italian covered road lead?

426. Jonathan has a guidebook to Corinth and its surrounding area. How are the best hotels and taverns recommended in this codex?
A. They are marked with a little symbol representing a house and courtyard
B. They are marked with the Greek letter alpha
C. They are marked with a little picture of Jupiter's thunderbolt

D. They are marked with the grinning head of a gorgon

427. On the road to Athens, the four friends come across a roadside shrine to Castor and Pollux. Which ONE of the following would an ancient traveller probably NOT offer at this kind of shrine?
A. Bunch of wildflowers
B. Apple
C. Tomato
D. Coin
E. Jewellery
F. Candle

428. In the town of Megara, near Athens, was the famous Fountain of Theagenes. According to Jonathan's guidebook – and Pausanias – what can you see embedded in its columns?
A. Seashells
B. Specks of gold
C. Jewels
D. Fossils

429. On the road from Corinth to Athens, travellers could sometimes see the tip of a spear gleaming far across the Saronic Gulf. The spear was held by a colossal statue which stood on the Acropolis of Athens? Whom did the statue represent?

430. If a Greek city-state won a great battle after following the Delphic oracle's advice, its leaders would often show their thanks by erecting a

building to hold the spoils of the conquered. There were many such buildings at Delphi. What were these buildings called?

431. Individuals as well as city-states could make dedications at Delphi. They often dedicated statues. Which ONE of the following do the friends NOT see in the sanctuary of Apollo at Delphi?
A. A colossal statue of Helios, the sun-god
B. A giant statue of a three-headed snake
C. A golden palm tree
D. A bronze wolf
E. An iron sculpture of Hercules

432. The Greeks believed the centre of the world was located in Delphi and they even pointed out a stone which resembled a giant navel. What did they call this navel-stone?

433. By Flavia's time (the late first century AD), Rome had spread beyond the city wall first built five hundred years earlier. What was the name of this wall?

434. As the friends walk to the Stables of the Greens in the Campus Martius, Aristo points out the *Pons Fabricius*, 'which leads to the Tiber Island'. What is a *pons*?

For the answers to these questions, turn to page 149.

RITES, RITUALS AND SUPERSTITIONS

435. Many Roman emperors were highly superstitious, Titus included. What causes Titus to invite Flavia and her friends to Rome at the beginning of *The Enemies of Jupiter*?

436. When Roman families celebrate the nine day festival of the Parentalia in February, they bring out the death masks of their ancestors. What are these death masks usually made of?

437. Where do family members go on the last day of the Parentalia?

438. According to Titus, what word is it bad luck to utter at banquets?

439. In *The Enemies of Jupiter*, the detectives arrive in Rome on the Ides of February, just in time for a Roman festival of fertility. Boys dressed in wolf-skins run through the streets of Rome, sprinkling women with blood. What is the name of this festival?

440. Because of the plague, Titus has been making sacrifices daily at the temples of two gods known for healing. Apollo is one of the gods. Who is the other?

441. When Titus sacrifices a bull on the Tiber Island, he wears something that a Roman priest does not usually wear – a wreath of leaves. He does this in honour of Coronis, Aesculapius's mother. What does her name mean?

442. Lupus steals a small votive object of clay to offer in the temple of Aesculapius. What is this votive shaped like?

443. In *The Aeneid*, the poet Virgil describes two gates through which dreams pass. True dreams pass through a gate made of horn. False dreams pass through a gate made of ....?

444. According to Jewish legend, which of these items is NOT stored in the Ark of the Covenant?
    A. An alabastron containing frankincense
    B. Aaron's rod
    C. A jar full of manna
    D. Two stone tablets, on which are carved the Ten Commandments

445. During the events at the arena, there was often a man dressed in black robes with a white mask who would finish off mortally wounded criminals or beast-fighters with a blow to the head. He was sometimes called ...., after the King of the Underworld.

446. The Jewish festival of Purim commemorates the victory of Queen Esther and the Jewish people

over those who would persecute them. What is the name of their chief persecutor?

447. At the beginning of *The Colossus of Rhodes*, Alma gives the four friends amulets, shaped like a boy's private parts. Aristo calls the amulets 'apotropaic', and says this word means to 'ward off' or 'turn away'. What do the apotropaic amulets ward off?

448. One of the festivals of Fors Fortuna, goddess of good fortune, was held three days after the midsummer solstice. What day is this?

449. After Nebuchadnezzar destroyed Solomon's Temple he sent many Jews into exile, to Babylon. Later some of the exiles returned to Jerusalem to build a new temple on the site of the first one. What did they call the new temple?

450. When Lupus sets sail in February AD 80, his secret goal is to find his mother. Before he leaves Ostia, he shapes an altar of sand on the beach and prays to the gods for success. What animal does he sacrifice on the sandy altar?

451. Beside the *Delphina*'s wooden swan's neck ornament is a small altar on which daily offerings for a good voyage will be made. To which god or goddess is this altar dedicated?

452. Flavia wonders if the *Delphina* might be haunted by lemures. What are lemures?

453. In Roman times, one of the Greek islands is known as the Island of Bald Men, because they believed that if a man set foot upon it he would lose his hair. What is the name of the island?

454. When cold blue fire surrounds Lupus's head at the end of a storm near Rhodes, the sailors believe it is a portent and that the gods have chosen Lupus for ....?

455. When the *Delphina* is fogbound and becalmed near Rhodes, Jonathan tells Flavia it is all her f ault because she said 'Nothing else ....'?

456. In the sanctuary of Helios on Rhodes, Lupus sees a tree which seems to be covered by a golden fleece. In fact it is covered with thousands of rectangular leaf-thin scraps of copper with prayers and wishes scratched on them. What is such a tree called?

457. On the island of Rhodes, Lupus wonders if it is a good or a bad omen when he sees two celestial objects together in the sky. What are they?

458. Near the prima meta of the Circus Maximus, Lupus finds a shrine to the god Consus. What is unusual about this shrine?

459. There was also a shrine on the actual track near Sentator Cornix's seats, and even today a road near the site of the Circus Maximus retains the name of the goddess to whom the shrine was dedicated. What was her name?

460. Between each of the starting gates of the Circus Maximus were plinths with the head of a god and his private parts, too. Lupus thinks them rude but Flavia explains they are to keep away evil. What are they called?

461. Flavia and her friends are given a lead curse tablet which was found buried near the Stables of the Greens. What was buried with the curse tablet?

462. Which ONE of the following is NOT a characteristic of the lead curse-tablet against the Greens?
A. It is written backwards
B. It is written with Hebrew letters
C. The language is Aramaic
D. It is written on both sides of the tablet
E. It invokes demons

463. Before dawn on the Nones of September, Senator Cornix leads his household in prayer to the household gods in his role of paterfamilias. What does he sprinkle on the coals that makes Flavia want to sneeze?

464. Urbanus is furious because his charioteers – 'the superstitious creatures' – have panicked: 'Someone has taken their ....'

For the answers to these questions, turn to page 150.

NUBIA–ISMS

Nubia's Latin is not yet fluent and she unintentionally says some strange things. Match what Nubia says with what is meant.

465. flem attic

466. tar pee un rock

467. my oh bees

468. eye school ape pee us

469. retee are ree

470. die lemon

471. apple tropic

472. you fee muss

473. pamoranic

A. A bird-loving Argonaut.

B. A charioteer

C. Cliff from which traitors are thrown

D. Men who fight with a net, trident and dagger

E. Boys who sprinkle horses and track with water at the races

F. One of the four humours

G. Mother of fourteen children and victim of hubris

H. Something that repels bad luck

I. Something which renders poison harmless

474. pro man tee uh	J.	Rule which precludes Delphi natives from queuing for the Pythia.
475. anti boat	K.	The god of healing
476. oar rigger	L.	A view which allows you to see all around
477. who bricks	M.	Overweening pride
478. sprinkly boys	N.	A difficult choice

For the answers to these questions, turn to page 151.

OUTTAKES

None of the following passages made it into the final version of the Roman Mysteries. Can you work out which of books seven to twelve each originally came from?

479. Flavia threw off the covers and crawled to the cedarwood chest at the foot of her bed. Scuto and Nipur both moved forward to help investigate, then retreated as tunics and pallas flew out and landed on the floor, bed and table. At last Flavia's head emerged. 'Here it is!' she cried. 'My ostraka box.'

    'What is ostraka box?' asked Nubia, sitting up.

    Flavia flopped on the end of Nubia's bed. 'When I was four years old, I begged pater to teach me to read, but he just laughed. So I tried to teach myself. Whenever I found a piece of broken pottery with writing on it, I saved it and tried to decipher it. And whenever I saw graffiti on the wall, I tried to copy it down. I used one of pater's old wax tablets,' she explained. 'One day he caught me copying some graffiti and he said that if I was so keen to learn to read, I had better start with something which was not rude and which was spelled correctly. So he started to teach me. And when I was eight he brought Aristo home to be my tutor. I showed Aristo my box full of clay pieces with writing on them and he said the word for broken pottery in Greek was *ostraka*. It was the first Greek word I learned. And somewhere—' she upturned the box so that two dozen ceramic pieces clattered onto Nubia's bedspread, '—somewhere is a fragment of a Greek wine-jug showing Pegasus the winged horse.'

480. Someone once told Flavia that when you are about to die your life unrolls before you like a painted scroll dropped on the floor. But as she stared into the jaws of the crocodile she did not see her whole life, only scenes. She saw herself at the age of three, placing flowers beside her mother's funeral urn in the Geminus family tomb. She saw herself aged four, copying out graffiti on an old wax tablet. Here she was aged five, throwing her arms around the furry neck of Scuto, her Saturnalia present. She saw Jonathan, Nubia and Lupus. And she saw the mountain erupting.

481. 'Is she asleep?' whispered Jonathan.

Lupus shrugged, and Nubia said, 'I do not know.'

In the pale light of morning Jonathan saw their eyes were red-rimmed, for they had been awake all night, helping the doctor.

'No,' said Flavia, without opening her eyes. 'I'm not asleep. I'm trying to imagine what it's like to be dead.'

Nubia, Jonathan and Lupus exchanged glances.

'I'm trying to imagine what it's like to be dead,' repeated Flavia. 'But I can't.'

482. Lupus sat on the beach of Ostia between two sand dunes.

It was a perfect spring day, warm and bright, with a gentle breeze that lifted the seagulls high in the blue sky. The plume of smoke from the lighthouse further up the coast showed that this breeze was coming from the northwest. Lupus hugged his knees to his chest and looked out at the ships moving over the glittering Tyrrhenian Sea. He saw dozens of sails, some square and some triangular; some striped and some plain; but all taking advantage of the perfect conditions.

As he watched them, Lupus remembered the promise he had made to himself the month before. He had silently vowed to take his ship and sail back to his mother as soon as the sailing season began.

The sailing season had begun a month ago. And he was still in Ostia.

Lupus stood and walked across the soft warm sand to the beach, to the place where the little waves hissed up on the shore. He dug his fingers into the damp sand and began to form it into a block as high and wide and deep as his forearm.

When he finished shaping the altar, Lupus looked around. He needed something that would bleed.

483. Nubia waited outside the Geminus family shrine and pulled her lionskin tighter round her shoulders. It was a pure blue day, and chilly. But it was not the cold that made her shiver.

It was the spirits of the dead.

Lemures, Flavia called them.

Other families were gathering here in the necropolis. Nubia watched them, the poorer ones pouring wine onto the ground and scattering salt, the rich ones disappearing into their family tombs. The recent fever had taken many, so the wails of grief were fresh and raw. Presently the mourners would depart, leaving flowers and honey cakes behind to console those who would never again gaze upon the blue sky.

484. 'Nubia?' whispered Flavia. 'Are you awake?'

A sleepy voice answered. 'Yes, I am awake.'

'Have you ever kissed a man?'

A pause. 'I have kissed my father and my brothers.'

'No. I mean a proper man. A man you like.'

'No. I am never kissing a man I like.'

'Who would you like your first kiss to be with?'

Silence. Then: 'You know who.'

'Aristo?'

'Yes,' said Nubia softly.

After a pause, Flavia said, 'Do you remember Flaccus?'

'Floppy?'

'Yes. Do you think . . . Have you ever thought about kissing him?'

'No,' said Nubia. 'I only want to kiss Aristo. He is the love of my life.'

Flavia sighed. 'Well, you'd better join the myriad other women in Ostia who love Aristo.' She rolled over and closed her eyes. 'I'm just glad *I'm* not in Aristo's queue.'

For the answers to these questions, turn to page 152.

GENERAL QUIZ

485. What word beginning with 'M' is the honey-sweetened wine which Romans often drank at the beginning of a meal?

486. Some scholars think Worcestershire sauce is the closest modern equivalent to the popular Roman sauce made from fermented fish entrails. What did the Roman's call their famous fish-sauce?

487. In Greek mythology, who was the Trojan son of the goddess Venus who escaped Troy with his father and son and eventually settled near the site of what would be Rome?

488. What was the name of Egypt's great port in Roman times, the home of a famous library and one of the Seven Wonders of the World?

489. There were no radiators in Roman times, so people used to put coals into a special type of metal bowl on legs. As the coals heated the bowl, it radiated heat and warmed the room. What do we call these coal-filled metal bowls on legs?

490. Brindisi is an Italian port on the heel of Italy's 'boot'. It was a port in Roman times, too. What was it called then?

491. When a doctor practised cautery in Roman times, what did he burn?

492. Porphyry comes from the Greek word for 'purple'. What was porphyry?

493. Near the Esquiline Hill in Rome was a poor, crowded and dangerous district whose name sounds a bit like 'suburbs'. What was the name for this dangerous district?

494. A mythological hero called Actaeon was hunting in the woods when he accidentally came upon a goddess bathing in a pond. Captivated by her beauty, he lingered to watch. When she caught him spying on her, she furiously turned him into a deer and caused his own hounds to tear him limb from limb. Who was the goddess?

495. What was cruel and unusual about the helmet that an andabata gladiator had to wear?

496. After her encounter with crocs, hippos and bears, Sisyphus gives Flavia a sleeping potion. When she wakes up late the next morning she complains that her 'mouth feels like the Cloaca Maxima'. What was the Cloaca Maxima?

497. Who was the mythological inventor who made the maze for the minotaur and wings for his son Icarus?

498. What creature's name means 'river-horse' in Greek?

499. The retiarius gladiator wore very little armour, just a metal belt and a galerus. Can you guess what a 'galerus' was?

500. What Latin word beginning with 'L' describes the man who trained gladiators?

501. Who was the beautiful daughter of Demeter, whom Pluto kidnapped and kept in the Underworld for six months of every year?

502. The 'vela' or 'velarium' helped people enjoy the games at the arena or the plays in the theatre, especially on hot days. What were they?

503. What Latin word beginning with 'P' describes a person of the highest Roman social class?

504. Who was the mythical prince of Troy who had to decide which of the three goddesses – Juno, Minerva or Venus – was the most beautiful?

505. According to some accounts a woman joined the heroes who sailed with Jason on the Argo. Her special skill was running fast. What was the fast heroine's name?

506. What word beginning with 'A' and meaning 'high city' in Greek was the name of the site of most of the monuments in Athens?

507. Which city-state of ancient Greece was famous for its fierce warriors who lived with the minimum of comfort?

508. What Latin word for 'prophetess' – beginning with 'S' – was the Roman equivalent of the Pythia in Greece?

509. Polydeuces was the Greek counterpart of which Roman demi-god?

510. The Greek demi-god Hypnos was often shown flying down to touch the foreheads of sleepy people with a special branch. What was he the god of?

511. What word beginning with 'T' – and coming from the Greek word meaning 'four' – is a small four-sided chip of stone, ivory, pottery or glass?

512. On what occasion would a Roman man wear a synthesis?

513. What Latin word beginning with 'P' is the refreshing drink made by adding vinegar to water, favoured by Roman soldiers and modest matrons because it is non-alcoholic?

514. The fulcrum was the curved part at the head of a dining couch. In which room of a Roman house would you often find three dining couches?

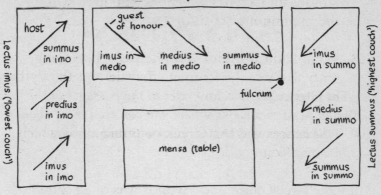

COUCHES IN A TRICLINIUM

Lectus medius ('middle couch')

Lectus imus ('lowest couch')

host

summus in imo

predius in imo

imus in imo

guest of honour

imus in medio

medius in medio

summus in medio

fulcrum

mensa (table)

imus in summo

medius in summo

summus in summo

Lectus summus ('highest couch')

515. What 'P'-word coming from the Latin word for 'little loaf' do we still use today to mean a moulded pill or lozenge?

For the answers to these questions, turn to page 152.

ANSWERS

The page numbers below refer to the passages in the Roman Mysteries books where you can read more about the background to the questions and answers.

MAP QUIZZES

1. Altar – C.
2. Anchor – J.
3. Artemon – F.
4. Deck-house – B.
5. Halyard – E.
6. Hull – H.
7. Lifts – K.
8. Mainmast – D.
9. Steering oars – A.
10. Tiller – G.

VILLA OF POLLIUS FELIX

11. Atrium – J.
12. Baths – D.
13. Entrance to the Secret Cove – K.
14. Library Tower – E.
15. Ornamental pool – F.
16. Shrine of Venus – C.
17. Slave quarters – H.
18. Stables – A.

19. Statue of Felix – B.
20. Terrace – G.

CIRCUS MAXIMUS

21. Carceres (starting gates) – G.
22. Dolphin markers – B.
23. Egg markers – J.
24. Linea alba – H.
25. Meta prima – E.
26. Obelisk of Augustus – A.
27. Shrine of Consus (underground) – C.
28. Shrine of Murcia – K.
29. Statue of Victory – F.
30. Temple of the Sun and Finishing Box – D.

THE ENEMIES OF JUPITER

31. Venison (p 1).
32. Because she hasn't had the fever yet (p 5).
33. C. Taking her temperature (pp 11-12).
34. A. Marjoram (p 12).
35. A. Sugar loaf (p 13).
36. A. Salt (p 15).
37. Overweening pride (p 16).
38. B. Water (pp 22-24).
39. A cupping vessel or 'bleeding cup' (p 21).
40. Fire (p 24).
41. Agathus (p 37).
42. The Capitoline Hill (p 50).
43. Latin (p 52).
44. Saffron (p 45).

45. Ivory (p 47).

46. Geese (p 50).

47. The Tarpeian Rock (p 51).

48. Josephus (p 53.)

49. The Tiber Island (p 57).

50. Augustus (p 59).

51. Apollo (p 49).

52. A cobra (p 89).

53. Julia (p 106).

54. The Ark of the Covenant (p109).

55. Nero Caesar (p 120).

56. Greek (p 114-115).

57. A. Kitten (p 120-121).

58. Cynthia (p 148).

59. B. The giant wave caused by the volcano (p 159).

60. Fire! (p 183).

ENTERTAINMENT IN ROMAN TIMES

61. Naufragium! (*The Charioteer of Delphi*, p 3)

62. Thirty-two. (A biga is a two-horsed chariot and there were four factions, so 4 chariots x 4 factions x 2 horses = 32.)

63. 250,000 – a quarter of a million!

64. F. Execution of criminals during breaks between events.

65. At the Stagnum (*The Gladiators from Capua*, p 20).

66. Carpophorus (*The Gladiators from Capua*, p 73).

67. A. Orange (*The Gladiators from Capua*, p 1).

68. C. Senators (*The Gladiators from Capua*, p 61).

69. A female beast-fighter (*The Gladiators from Capua*, p 76).

70. A retiarius (*The Gladiators from Capua*, p 52).

71. A murmillo (*The Gladiators from Capua*, pp 144 and 209).

72. Captain (*The Charioteer of Delphi*, p 228).
73. D. A steel sword. (Gladiators were occasionally given wooden swords, but never real ones!)
74. C. Hippopotamus (*The Gladiators from Capua*, p 97).
75. Jerusalem (*The Enemies of Jupiter*, p 158).
76. B. 1,000 (*The Charioteer of Delphi*, p 24).
77. He is asking for mercy (*The Gladiators from Capua*, pp 139-140).
78. 'Habet!' (*The Gladiators from Capua*, p 158, etc).
79. A gladius (*The Gladiators from Capua*, p 159).
80. Seven (*The Charioteer of Delphi*, p 73).
81. A. It makes it easier to run off the track if he is thrown out of the chariot.
82. They blindfolded them (*The Gladiators from Capua*, p 90).
83. A secutor (*The Gladiators from Capua*, p 152).
84. Missio (*The Gladiators from Capua*, p 158).
85. Julius Caesar (*The Gladiators from Capua*, p 149).
86. Swallows (*The Colossus of Rhodes*, pp 51-52).
87. C. Chariot racing (*The Charioteer of Delphi*, p 23).
88. Applause (the highest kind) (*The Charioteer of Delphi*, p 107).
89. Leave their lanes (*The Charioteer of Delphi*, p 66).
90. A blindfolded slave.

LOOKING GOOD IN ROMAN TIMES

91. B. Starts using hair oil (p 6).
92. Susannah has perfectly straight hair (*The Enemies of Jupiter*, p 39).
93. Her name is branded on her forehead (*The Enemies of Jupiter*, p 41).
94. Honey (*The Sirens of Surrentum*, p 37).

95. Her tan (*The Sirens of Surrentum*, p 14).

96. Palaestra (*The Sirens of Surrentum*, p 14).

97. Polished bronze or silver (*The Sirens of Surrentum*, p 22).

98. Flavia-sized (*The Sirens of Surrentum*, p 22).

99. Grey (*The Sirens of Surrentum*, p 22).

100. Doe (*The Sirens of Surrentum*, p 26).

101. A. Eyes too small (*The Sirens of Surrentum*, p 38).

102. B. Too high (*The Sirens of Surrentum*, p 38).

103. Dull (*The Sirens of Surrentum*, p 38).

104. D. Having fresh breath (*The Sirens of Surrentum*, p 38).

105. A. Mouthwash made of urine and wine (*The Sirens of Surrentum*, pp 45, 48, 167, etc).

106. Monkey-legs (*The Sirens of Surrentum*, p 47).

107. C. Charcoal (*The Sirens of Surrentum*, p 56).

108. A. Bathe in asses' milk (*The Sirens of Surrentum*, p 58, etc).

109. C. Hare (*The Sirens of Surrentum*, p 37).

110. Belladonna (*The Sirens of Surrentum*, p 75).

111. Warm grey mud (*The Sirens of Surrentum*, p 138).

112. C. Diamond nose-studs (*The Sirens of Surrentum*, p 123).

113. D. Goat-hair toupees (*The Sirens of Surrentum*, p 124).

114. 18 years old (*The Sirens of Surrentum*, p 68).

115. Minerva (*The Sirens of Surrentum*, pp 67-68).

116. E. Mauve (*The Charioteer of Delphi*, p 20).

117. An umbrella hat (*The Charioteer of Delphi*, p 104).

118. Kohl (dark eye-liner) (*The Charioteer of Delphi*, p 21 and elsewhere).

119. E. Towel (*The Charioteer of Delphi*, p 25).

120. Castor (*The Charioteer of Delphi*, pp 88-89).

THE GLADIATORS FROM CAPUA

121. Rome (p 3).
122. Isola Sacra (p 3).
123. A eulogy (p 4).
124. Potsherd Mountain (p 25).
125. Caecilius. His full name is Aulus Caecilius Cornix (p 16).
126. D. Clivus Scauri (p 23).
127. Dust from the desert (p 31).
128. Beast-fighters (p 32).
129. Siwa (p 35).
130. Palus (pp 167, 210).
131. Monobaz (p 42).
132. Water organ (pp 48-49).
133. The Ludus Aureus (p 51).
134. Spartacus (p 52).
135. The attic (p 59).
136. Baiae (p 51).
137. B. Bloodlust (p 65).
138. A tightrope-walking elephant (p 67).
139. Savage (p 69).
140. Walnut juice (p 97).
141. Fork (the two-pronged wooden fork acted as a yoke, forcing the criminal to look up) (pp 78-79).
142. A boar (p 88).
143. E. A sponge-on-a-stick (p 92).
144. A garland (p 114).
145. Archery (p 118-119).
146. Martial (p 122).
147. She cuts her finger (p 135).

148. A mist of perfume sprayed from above (p 148).
149. Pantherus (p 151).
150. Sextus (which means 'six') (p 151-152).

KILL OR CURE

151. Spring (*The Enemies of Jupiter*, p 23).
152. Diaulus (*The Enemies of Jupiter*, pp 76-79).
153. Cosmus (*The Enemies of Jupiter*, pp 79-82).
154. Urine (*The Enemies of Jupiter*, pp 90-91).
155. C. Cheese (*The Enemies of Jupiter*, p 89).
156. Smintheus (*The Enemies of Jupiter*, p 86).
157. B. Drinking wine (*The Enemies of Jupiter*, pp 93-96).
158. Water (*The Enemies of Jupiter*, p 12).
159. B. Bled every other day (*The Enemies of Jupiter*, pp 74-75).
160. C. Bathing (*The Enemies of Jupiter*, p 81).
161. Snorteum (*The Enemies of Jupiter*, p 22).
162. Ephedron (*The Enemies of Jupiter*, p 87).
163. Asclepion (*The Enemies of Jupiter*, p 86).
164. Snake Island (*The Enemies of Jupiter*, p 61).
165. He urinates on it (*The Colossus of Rhodes*, p 71).
166. Mastic (*The Colossus of Rhodes*, pp 78-79).
167. Cobwebs.
168. Amnesia (*The Fugitive from Corinth*, p 28).
169. Wolfsbane (*The Sirens of Surrentum*, p 75).
170. B. Oleander (*The Sirens of Surrentum*, p 79).
171. C. To sweeten the breath (*The Sirens of Surrentum*, p 80).
172. D. Arsenic (*The Sirens of Surrentum*, p 72-73).
173. Mithridates (*The Sirens of Surrentum*, p 84).
174. A. Rose petals (*The Sirens of Surrentum*, p 85).
175. Socrates (*The Sirens of Surrentum*, p 159).
176. Feather (*The Sirens of Surrentum*, p 133).

177. C. Rolling naked in the snow (*The Sirens of Surrentum*, pp 75 ff).
178. B. Swallowing burning coals (*The Sirens of Surrentum*, p 116, etc).
179. Venus (*The Sirens of Surrentum*, p 206).
180. Liquid medicine given by mouth (*The Charioteer of Delphi*, p 38).

THE COLOSSUS OF RHODES

181. Venalicius (p 4).
182. Greek.
183. He owns it (p 10).
184. Valerius (p 14).
185. D. Muscular (p 15).
186. Bubbles (p 18).
187. Iota (p 19).
188. Pigeons (pp 50, etc).
189. Tigris (p 21).
190. Zetes (p 23).
191. Lupus (p 24).
192. Floppy (p 25).
193. C. Sacks of grain (p 26).
194. Charbybdis (p 34).
195. Lemons (p 32).
196. The Argonautica (p 201).
197. The *Medea* (p 43).
198. B. That he is a woman. (pp 48, etc).
199. B. Varro (p 57).
200. D. Falernian wine (pp 56, etc).
201. Patmos (pp 93-94).
202. C. Killer whale (pp 38, etc).

203. Aphrodite (p 104).
204. Cnidos (p 126).
205. It fell down in an earthquake (p 133).
206. The rays of the sun (p 173, etc).
207. Boots (pp 155-156).
208. B. Street of the Coppersmiths (p 136).
209. His life (p 188).
210. D. Marble blocks from Cnidos (p 193).

TRAVEL AND TRANSPORT

211. Our sea.
212. The Tyrrhenian Sea (*The Colossus of Rhodes*, p 70).
213. Claudius.
214. D. Vanilla from Yucatan. (First-century Romans did not reach Central America.)
215. A sea voyage (*The Colossus of Rhodes*, p 2).
216. The Seven Wonders of the World (*The Colossus of Rhodes*, p 14).
217. B. Setting sail on an odd day of the month (*The Colossus of Rhodes*, pp 6-7).
218. The lustratio (*The Colossus of Rhodes*, pp 7, 39, 204).
219. By the plume of smoke rising from Ostia's lighthouse (*The Colossus of Rhodes*, p 7).
220. The harbourmaster (*The Colossus of Rhodes*, p 6).
221. The Cygnet (*The Colossus of Rhodes*, p 16).
222. D. If the ship is passing between clashing rocks.
223. The tiller (*The Colossus of Rhodes*, p 12).
224. The stern (*The Colossus of Rhodes*, p 11).
225. Capri (*The Colossus of Rhodes*, pp 29, 198).
226. By the stars (*The Colossus of Rhodes*, p 39).
227. Cape Malea (*The Colossus of Rhodes*, p 45).

228. The diolkos (*The Colossus of Rhodes*, p 42).

229. D. Zephyrus (*The Colossus of Rhodes*, p 57).

230. Everybody dines together (*The Colossus of Rhodes*, p 58).

231. C. Abafts.

232. A. The artemon (*The Colossus of Rhodes*, pp 121, 197).

233. St. Paul.

234. His hair.

235. The mule (*The Fugitive from Corinth*, p 54).

236. B. An imperial messenger (*The Fugitive from Corinth*, p77).

237. B. It uses the three colour printing method (*The Fugitive from Corinth,* p 41).

238. Procrustes (*The Fugitive from Corinth*, p 44).

239. Mystagogus (*The Fugitive from Corinth*, p 107).

240. B. Apollo ashtrays (*The Fugitive from Corinth*, p 106).

THE FUGITIVE FROM CORINTH

241. Aristo (p 4).

242. Neptune.

243. Corinth (p 209).

244. Hospitium (p 1).

245. C. He asks for oil and vinegar (pp 17-18).

246. A gladiator (p 23).

247. Myrtilla (p 27).

248. Pepper (p 54).

249. Bull (p 42).

250. Aegeus (p 42).

251. Sinis the Pine-Bender (p 43).

252. Chamber pot (p 50).

253. Evil Stairs (p 57).

254. A turtle (p 68).

255. Persian (p 68).

256. D. The Scylla (pp 75, 80, etc).
257. B. They fire poisoned arrows (p 80).
258. Clytemnestra (p 79).
259. Delphi (p 80).
260. C. Corinth (p 78).
261. Cow land (p 86).
262. Corinth (p 88).
263. The Split (p 94).
264. Pythia (p 96).
265. The Castalian Spring (pp 103-105).
266. Temenos (p 221).
267. Death (p 134).
268. E. Priests of Isis, bald and with long white robes (p 160).
269. A. A colossal bronze statue of Athena; it is made of gold and ivory (pp 172-173).
270. D. Potato (p 202).

ILLUSTRATED ARISTO'S SCROLL

271. 3.A
272. 15.G
273. 13.L
274. 14.O
275. 7.J
276. 6.K
277. 12.N
278. 4.H
279. 8.C
280. 9.B
281. 1.I
282. 10.F
283. 11.E

284. 5.D
285. 2.M

THE SIRENS OF SURRENTUM

286. Poison (p 5).
287. Lavinia (p 6).
288. A container for fattening dormice (p 108).
289. Ajax (p 14).
290. C. Noble vinegar (p 216).
291. Voluptua (pp 23-25).
292. D. Philodemus (p 40).
293. A. Calypso.
294. D. A make-up kit (p 56).
295. Suetonius (pp 85, 224).
296. Bird-lime (p 39).
297. A verna (p 45).
298. B. Freedom from passion (pp 48, 151, etc).
299. E. Sappho (p 48, etc).
300. Blond (or golden) (p 97).
301. Dessert or pudding (p 57).
302. Odysseus (p 60).
303. A. Ambrosium – made of vanilla, eucalyptus, hibiscus and musk (p 65, etc).
304. Locusta (p 85).
305. Pugnate! (p 92).
306. Agrippina (p 110).
307. Lucan (p 115).
308. Seneca (pp 115-116).
309. Oysters (p 119).
310. Virtue (p 121).
311. C. Charity (p 150).

312. A sponge-stick (p 151).

313. A. Lucilius (p 155).

314. She is clothed, not nude (p 212).

315. D. She was barefoot at the time (p 225).

QUIPS AND QUOTATIONS

316. Pandora's box (*The Enemies of Jupiter*, p 45).

317. Hearts (*The Enemies of Jupiter*, p 103).

318. Memento mori (*The Enemies of Jupiter*, p 15).

319. Dis manibus (*The Gladiators from Capua*, p 4).

320. Know thyself (*The Fugitive from Corinth*, p 110).

321. The eruption of Vesuvius (*The Sirens of Surrentum*, p 17).

322. Death (*The Enemies of Jupiter*, p 169).

323. Deus ex machina (*The Gladiators from Capua*, p 123).

324. Under a rose (*The Sirens of Surrentum*, p 158).

325. Leisure rather than business (*The Sirens of Surrentum*, p 150).

326. Ovid (*The Charioteer of Delphi*, p 13).

327. Jupiter (*The Enemies of Jupiter*, p 76).

328. Cheese (*The Enemies of Jupiter*, p 89).

329. Ascletario (*The Enemies of Jupiter*, p 55).

330. 'Tomorrow! Tomorrow!' (*The Enemies of Jupiter*, p 193).

331. Dry land (*The Gladiators from Capua*, p 125).

332. Boat (*The Colossus of Rhodes*, p 31).

333. Porridge (*The Fugitive from Corinth*, p 93).

334. Fratricide (*The Fugitive from Corinth*, p 111).

335. Me (*The Fugitive from Corinth*, p 120).

336. Croesus (*The Fugitive from Corinth*, p 97).

337. She cries (*The Fugitive from Corinth*, p 207).

338. Boar (*The Sirens of Surrentum*, p 49).

339. The Odyssey (*The Sirens of Surrentum*, p 61).

340. Sirens (*The Sirens of Surrentum*, p 104).

341. Baiae (*The Sirens of Surrentum*, p 108).

342. God (*The Sirens of Surrentum*, p 117).

343. Hurt (*The Sirens of Surrentum*, pp 151-2).

344. Truth (*The Sirens of Surrentum*, p 204).

345. Death (*The Sirens of Surrentum*, p 174).

MYTHS AND LEGENDS

346. Medusa.

347. Fire (*The Enemies of Jupiter*, p 34).

348. Pecks at his liver (*The Enemies of Jupiter*, p 36).

349. Hope (*The Enemies of Jupiter*, p 35).

350. Leto (*The Enemies of Jupiter*, p 49).

351. Leda.

352. A snake (*The Enemies of Jupiter*, p 61).

353. A thunderbolt (*The Enemies of Jupiter*, p 61).

354. B. The man-eating horse (was one of Hercules' labours, not Theseus's).

355. Jupiter (or Zeus) (*The Gladiators from Capua*, pp 81-82).

356. Oedipus (*The Enemies of Jupiter*, p 16).

357. A. The Cyclops (*The Colossus of Rhodes*, p 19-20).

358. Ithaca.

359. Dido (*The Sirens of Surrentum*, pp 117-8).

360. Odysseus (*The Sirens of Surrentum*, p 60).

361. Pegasus, the winged horse (*The Charioteer of Delphi*, p 14).

362. Neptune (or Poseidon) (*The Charioteer of Delphi*, p 15).

363. Minerva (or Athena) (*The Charioteer of Delphi*, p 15).

364. D. Eyes of a wolf (*The Charioteer of Delphi* pp 1, 15, etc).

365. They got boils and tumours (*The Enemies of Jupiter*, p 111).

366. Orpheus (*The Gladiators from Capua*, pp 105-110).

THE CHARIOTEER OF DELPHI

395. D. A horse from each faction was sacrificed to Neptune (p 58).
396. B. They are gilded (p 67).
397. She is Victory (p 66).
398. Canal (p 72).
399. The Whites (p 73).
400. Boars' dung (p 90).
401. A trumpet (p 92).
402. Britannicus (p 105).
403. The Blues (p 106).
404. F. The statue of Diana on the central barrier represents the moon (p 73).

ARCHITECTURE

405. In vertical stripes – red and white in this case (*The Enemies of Jupiter*, p 50).
406. Triangular (*The Enemies of Jupiter*, p 50).
407. Black (*The Enemies of Jupiter*, p 51).
408. The Forum Boarium (*The Enemies of Jupiter*, p 58; *The Charioteer of Delphi*, p 25).
409. D. Fierce watchdog chained outside (*The Gladiators from Capua*, p 164).
410. An obelisk (*The Enemies of Jupiter*, p 58).
411. A school for gladiators (*The Gladiators from Capua*, p 165).
412. Cone-shaped (*The Gladiators from Capua*, p 33).
413. Three.
414. A. Doric (*The Gladiators from Capua*, p 30).
415. The altar (*The Enemies of Jupiter*, p 164).
416. The abaton (*The Enemies of Jupiter*, p 62).
417. Halicarnassus (*The Colossus of Rhodes*, p 190).
418. Alexandria.

419. Artemis (or Diana).

420. The gold and ivory statue of Zeus (*The Colossus of Rhodes*, p 14).

421. The Great Pyramid.

422. The Hanging Gardens of Babylon.

423. That it straddles the harbour, with a leg on either side (*The Colossus of Rhodes*, p 133).

424. C. A fountain dedicated to Orpheus (*The Fugitive from Corinth*, p 36).

425. Felix's (*The Fugitive from Corinth*, p 36).

426. A. They are marked with a little symbol representing a house and courtyard (*The Fugitive from Corinth*, p 42).

427. C. Tomato (*The Fugitive from Corinth*, p 69).

428. A. Seashells (*The Fugitive from Corinth*, p 73).

429. Athena (*The Fugitive from Corinth*, p 68).

430. Treasuries (*The Fugitive from Corinth*, p109).

431. A. A colossal statue of Helios, the sun-god (*The Fugitive from Corinth*, pp 109-110, etc).

432. The omphalos (*The Fugitive from Corinth*, p 98).

433. The Servian Wall (*The Charioteer of Delphi*, p 25).

434 A bridge (*The Charioteer of Delphi*, p 26).

RITES, RITUALS AND SUPERSTITIONS

435. A dream (*The Enemies of Jupiter*, pp 44-45).

436. Wax (*The Enemies of Jupiter*, p 14).

437. The family tombs (*The Enemies of Jupiter*, p 14).

438. 'Fire' (*The Enemies of Jupiter*, pp 94-95).

439. The Lupercalia (*The Enemies of Jupiter*, p 209).

440. Aesculapius (*The Enemies of Jupiter*, p 44).

441. 'Garland' or 'crown' (*The Enemies of Jupiter*, p 65).

442. A tongue (*The Enemies of Jupiter*, p 68).

443. Ivory (*The Enemies of Jupiter*, p 102).

444. A. An alabastron containing frankincense (*The Enemies of Jupiter*, p 110).

445. Pluto (or Hades) (*The Gladiators from Capua*, p 84).

446. Haman (*The Enemies of Jupiter*, p 157).

447. Bad luck or evil(*The Colossus of Rhodes*, p 2).

448. 24 June [NOT 24 July as in Aristo's Scroll!].

449. The Second Temple (*The Enemies of Jupiter*, p 117).

450. A pigeon (*The Colossus of Rhodes*, p 5).

451. Venus (*The Colossus of Rhodes*, p 16).

452. The spirits of the dead (*The Colossus of Rhodes*, p 39).

453. Myconos (*The Colossus of Rhodes*, p 67).

454. 'Some great task' (*The Colossus of Rhodes*, p 127).

455. '...could go wrong' (*The Colossus of Rhodes*, p 131).

456. A votive tree (*The Colossus of Rhodes*, pp 160-161).

457. The sun and the moon (*The Colossus of Rhodes*, p 159).

458. It is underground (*The Charioteer of Delphi*, pp 157–158).

459. Murcia (*The Charioteer of Delphi*, p 59).

460. Herms (*The Charioteer of Delphi*, p 70).

461. A headless rooster (*The Charioteer of Delphi*, p 85).

462. D. It is written on both sides of the tablet (*The Charioteer of Delphi*, p 85).

463. Incense (*The Charioteer of Delphi*, p 93).

464. Idols (*The Charioteer of Delphi*, p 98*).

NUBIA-ISMS

465. F. Phlegmatic. (*The Enemies of Jupiter*, p 24).

466. C. Tarpeian Rock. (*The Enemies of Jupiter*, p 51).

467. G. Niobe. (*The Enemies of Jupiter*, p 51).

468. K. Aesculapius. (*The Enemies of Jupiter*, p 60*).

469. D. Retiarii. (*The Gladiators from Capua*, p 51).

470. N. Dilemma. (*The Gladiators from Capua*, p 162).

471. H. Apotropaic. (*The Colossus of Rhodes*, p 2).

472. A. Euphemus. (*The Colossus of Rhodes*, p 26).

473. L. Panoramic. (*The Fugitive from Corinth*, p 67).

474. J. Promanteia. (*The Fugitive from Corinth*, p 114).

475. I. Antidote. (*The Sirens of Surrentum*, p 71).

476. B. Aurgia. (*The Charioteer of Delphi*, p 6).

477. M. Hubris. (*The Enemies of Jupiter*, p 16).

478. E. Sparsores. (*The Charioteer of Delphi*, p 34).

OUTTAKES

479. *The Charioteer of Delphi*

480. *The Gladiators from Capua*

481. *The Fugitive from Corinth*

482. *The Colossus of Rhodes*

483. *The Enemies of Jupiter*

484. *The Sirens of Surrentum*

GENERAL QUIZ

485. Mulsum (*The Enemies of Jupiter*, p 210).

486. Garum (*The Enemies of Jupiter*, p 207).

487. Aeneas (*The Enemies of Jupiter*, p 203).

488. Alexandria (*The Enemies of Jupiter*, p 203).

489. Braziers (or tripods) (*The Enemies of Jupiter*, p 204).

490. Brindisium (*The Enemies of Jupiter*, p 205).

491. Human flesh (*The Enemies of Jupiter*, p 205).

492. A kind of rock from Egypt (*The Enemies of Jupiter*, p 211).

493. The subura (*The Enemies of Jupiter*, p 213).

494. Diana (or Artemis) (*The Gladiators from Capua*, p 203).

495. It had no eyeholes! (*The Gladiators from Capua*, p 203).
496. Romes' main sewer (*The Gladiators from Capua*, pp 184, 204).
497. Daedalus (*The Gladiators from Capua*, pp 87, 205).
498. Hippopotamus (*The Gladiators from Capua*, p 40).
499. A shoulder-guard (*The Gladiators from Capua*, p 206).
500. Lanista (*The Gladiators from Capua*, pp 166, 208).
501. Persephone (*The Gladiators from Capua*, p 210).
502. Awnings to give shade (*The Gladiators from Capua*, p 214).
503. Patrician (*The Colossus of Rhodes*, p 205).
504. Paris (*The Colossus of Rhodes*, p 205).
505. Atalanta (*The Colossus of Rhodes*, p 198).
506. Acropolis (*The Fugitive from Corinth*, p 209).
507. Sparta (*The Fugitive from Corinth*, p 220).
508. Sibyl (*The Fugitive from Corinth*, p 89).
509. Pollux (*The Fugitive from Corinth*, p 218).
510. Sleep (*The Fugitive from Corinth*, p 215).
511. Tessera (*The Sirens of Surrentum*, p 256).
512. To a dinner party (usually a casual one) (*The Sirens of Surrentum*, p 256).
513. Posca (*The Sirens of Surrentum*, p 253).
514. Triclinium (*The Sirens of Surrentum*, p 30).
515. Pastille (*The Sirens of Surrentum*, p 252).

ABOUT THE CONTRIBUTORS

James Beagon is fourteen years old. After reading the first book, he googled Roman Mysteries, and discovered the RM forum, which is still going today, administered by, among others, James and Roo (who contributed to the first *Quiz Book*). Jonathan is James's favourite character: 'He's the funniest, and in my opinion, has some of the best lines in the books. He's also asthmatic, like myself.' His favourite book in the series is *The Gladiators From Capua*. James says, 'I particularly like the scene where Flavia is stranded on the island with the bear, surrounded by water filled with crocodiles and hippos.'

Libby Coates is thirteen years old. Her favourite Roman Mystery is *The Twelve Tasks Of Flavia Gemina*, 'because the plot is very exciting and different'. Perhaps her favourite character is Sisyphus, for his youthful aspect on life. 'The best part in all the books,' according to Libby, 'is towards the beginning of *The Dolphins Of Laurentum*, where Jonathan and Lupus made a hole in their bedroom wall, creating a way to get between the two houses in secret. I've always dreamed of having that kind of thing in my bedroom. But I don't live on the town wall, sadly.'

Andrew Downey is Head of Classics at Westminster Upper School in London. He has also lived and taught in Italy, the north of England and south Wales. He has written a book of and on Latin Plays and he holds a Latin Play competition each year for schools in London. 'I enjoyed *The Gladiators from Capua* most (particularly for this use of Roman sources), but,' he says, *'The Charioteer of Delphi* is close to my heart as I hold chariot races in my lessons (on the board!) towards the end of each term. I admire the bravery of Jonathan.'

Errin Riley is eleven years old and a big fan of the Roman Mysteries. Her claim to fame is that she was auditioned and selected to be the official 'CBBC Spy' and reporter on the set of the TV series of the Roman Mysteries! Of her experience, Errin said, 'It was incredible. I couldn't believe how authentic all the Roman ships looked. The cast looked just like real Romans! . . . The best interview I did was with one of the pirates. We talked about Roman pirates and then he kidnapped me! You'll have to watch to find out how I escaped!'

And about the series' author, Caroline Lawrence . . .

Caroline Lawrence is a Californian who came to England to study Classics and has now lived in the UK longer than she lived in the US. Her favourite Roman Mystery of the second six is *The Sirens of Surrentum*, because she loves romance as well as action. Her favourite character is Flavia Gemina, because 'Flavia is a bossy know-it-all like me, but also a truth-seeker.'

THE·ROMAN·MYSTERIES

I THE THIEVES OF OSTIA

In the bustling, cosmopolitan port of Ostia, near Rome, a killer is at large. He is trying to silence the watchdogs. Flavia Gemina and her three new friends – Jonathan, Lupus and Nubia – follow the trail to find out why.

II THE SECRETS OF VESUVIUS

The four friends are staying near Pompeii, and trying to solve a strange riddle, when Mount Vesuvius erupts and they must flee for their lives. A thrilling account of one of the greatest natural disasters of all time.

III THE PIRATES OF POMPEII

The four friends discover that children are being kidnapped from the camps where hundreds of refugees are sheltering after the eruption of Vesuvius, and proceed to solve the mystery of the pirates of Pompeii.

IV THE ASSASSINS OF ROME

Jonathan disappears and his friends trace him to the Golden House of the Emperor Nero in Rome, where they learn the terrible story of what happened to his family in Jerusalem – and face a deadly assassin.

V THE DOLPHINS OF LAURENTUM

Off the coast of Laurentum, near Ostia, is a sunken wreck full of treasure. The friends are determined to retrieve it – but so is someone else. An exciting adventure which reveals the secret of Lupus's past.

VI THE TWELVE TASKS
OF FLAVIA GEMINA

It's December AD 79, and time for the Saturnalia festival, when anything goes. There's a lion on the loose in Ostia – and Flavia has reason to suspect the motives of a Roman widow who is interested in her father.

VII THE ENEMIES OF JUPITER

Emperor Titus summons the children to help him find the mysterious enemy who seeks to destroy Rome through plague and fire. Jonathan is distracted by a secret mission of his own, and suddenly everything gets terrifyingly out of control.

VIII THE GLADIATORS FROM CAPUA

March AD 80. In Rome, the Emperor Titus has announced that there will be a hundred days of games to open his new Flavian amphitheatre (now known as the Colosseum). A heart-pounding behind-the-scenes account of gladiator fights, executions and beast fights makes this one of the most exciting Roman Mysteries yet.

IX THE COLOSSUS OF RHODES

Spring AD 80. The sailing season has begun. Lupus decides to see if his mother is still alive and to follow his uncle's dying wish. The friends sail to the island of Rhodes, site of one of the seven wonders of the ancient world . . . and base of a criminal mastermind!

X THE FUGITIVE FROM CORINTH

May AD 80. Flavia and her three friends, Jonathan, Nubia and Lupus are in Cenchrea, the eastern harbour of Corinth, the hometown of Aristo, their tutor. But Aristo tells them he is not coming back with them this time. Later, there is a commotion, and the children find a blood-soaked Aristo crouched over Flavia's father, who has been stabbed. The children set off for Delphi in pursuit of Aristo . . .

XI THE SIRENS OF SURRENTUM

June AD 80. It's summer in the Bay of Naples – time for fun and relaxation. The four detectives are staying at the luxurious Villa Limona with Pulchra and her family. But there's a rotten core beneath the beauty. A famous murder was committed here once, and now Pulchra's mother claims someone is trying to poison her. Faced with many distractions, can the four friends find the culprit?

XII THE CHARIOTEER OF DELPHI

September AD 80. A famous racehorse has gone missing just days before the important events at the Circus Maximus.

Flavia and her friends are recruited to find the horse, but are soon embroiled in the dangerous and competitive world of the rival chariot-racing factions. Someone is trying to sabotage the Greens – is it an enemy from a rival faction, or could it be an inside job?

XIII THE SLAVE-GIRL FROM JERUSALEM

December AD 80. Ostia is gripped by a case of triple murder. The defendant seems the least likely villain – a tragic and beautiful slave-girl with a haunted past – and an important destiny. Who will defend the slave-girl, and is she really innocent? Join the four detectives in their race to find the truth before the verdict is decided.

TRIMALCHIO'S FEAST AND OTHER MINI-MYSTERES

Some of the Roman Mysteries pick up on the cliffhanger ending of the previous mystery. But often, a month or two passes between adventures. Lots of fans of the series ask Caroline what Flavia and her friends were doing during the in-between times. Others want to know what happened to characters met in earlier stories. This collection of mini-mysteries, each complete in itself, will help fill in those gaps, and maybe even answer some of *your* questions!

To find out more about Caroline Lawrence
and the Roman Mysteries visit

www.romanmysteries.com